FICTION

WWW.INDEPENDENTLEGIONS.COM

MICHAEL GRAY BAUGHAN

THE ANA LOG
& OTHER ANOMALIES

STORIES

ISBN: 979-12-80713-54-4
NOVEMBER 2022

RECIPIENT OF HWA SPECIALTY PRESS AWARD

THE ANA LOG
& OTHER ANOMALIES

CONTENTS

MICHAEL GRAY BAUGHAN

THE ANA LOG
& OTHER ANOMALIES

Continuing Ed

Night comes early when Graham's sudden right turn throws a forested ridge in front of the sunset. While he feathers the accelerator and twists the wheel back and forth to dodge a few offroad hazards, Finn makes a practice pull on the passenger door latch. Somewhere several maneuvers behind them, Finn's friend Petey is still backtracking to the spot where Graham managed to lose him. With any luck he will get lost and give up. Graham will happily give these edgy zoomers props for attempting the precaution, but he sure as hell isn't letting anyone uninvited tag along tonight.

Inside the tunnel of visibility carved by the old Chevy's headlights, the white poplars flash by like pale faces on a passing subway car. The old logging road narrows and narrows until thornbushes are bending beneath the truck's brush guard and raking their nails along its rust-eaten belly. Finn sits stiff and silent, his hand still curled around the latch. Graham has noticed the threat this poses by this point, and he hopes the kid has thought it through. Ejecting now will only leave him injured and lost. Not to mention deprived of the royal mind blowing that Graham promised him at the outset.

"You can take that off now," Graham says when he finally coasts to a stop.

Finn yanks down the blindfold and exhales like it covered his mouth. "Where the fuck are we?" The tattooed wound curling up and around his neck looks too realistic for Graham's tastes, especially the way its flexes when he speaks.

"I'm not going to tell you that. And even if I did, you'd never find your way out of here without me." The big man drives home the point by looping the long chain holding his truck keys over his head and tucking them under his beard.

Finn flinches when Graham suddenly leans across the bench seat and pops open the glove box.

"Put your phone in there."

"Why?"

"Because I said so."

"You watched me turn it off!"

"Yeah, and I can't have you turning it back on when I'm not paying attention and sneaking pictures or tracking us with your GPS, okay? I'm happy to renegotiate the terms for next time. If there is a next time."

Finn sighs and complies. "This better be worth it. What if it gets stolen?"

"Trust me." Graham slams the battered latch until it catches. "The only thing out here besides us doesn't need a phone to communicate."

Bait dangled, Graham heads around back and drops the tailgate. The kid takes a minute to join him there, but once he does Graham relaxes a bit. If the kid is intrigued enough to walk into these woods voluntarily, he might have a shot after all. They both grab their packs and Finn follows Graham through the first line of trees and onto a trail Graham knows well enough to follow in the dark.

***

"You ever heard of the term *genius loci*?" Graham says after they've been walking a few minutes in silence.

"I don't know," Finn hedges. "Maybe?"

"Deep time?"

"Is that anything like bullet time?"

"No. If anything it's the opposite. How about Spiritualism?"

"Ghost photos and séances and shit?"

"Bingo. Nobody talks about it much anymore, but it was pretty big in these parts around the turn of the century. The previous century, I mean."

"Total bullshit, though, right? You showed us in class how they faked those photos."

"Did I?" During the time he taught the class on old photography techniques at the Arts Center, Graham was quite literally running on fumes after double shifts running the developers at the only film lab left in town. "Not all of them were con artists, though."

Finn just waits, noncommittal.

"You asked where we are. I won't tell you that, not in any way you can map, but I can tell you a hundred years ago all this land was owned by one family. They made their fortune logging a big chunk of it, then coasted for a while. The family dwindled and sort of fell apart during the Depression. The forest came back. Last of them was a crazy spinster by the name of Stella."

"Please don't tell me you brought me all the way out here for some kind of Blair Witch bullshit."

Graham doesn't blame the kid for being this cynical. He spoke with the same cockiness his first time out here as well. "You know that creepy old building down the street from the Arts Center? The one with the animal heads running around the second story like gargoyles?"

"Yeah," Finn says. "One of my friends calls it Noah's Ark of the Covenant."

"Stella had that built to show off her collection of exotic specimens."

"No shit?" Finn says.

"No shit. I dug up an old pamphlet advertising the displays. Fiji Mermaids in the powder room, wooly mammoth in the lobby. Even had a mutant chimp in a big glass case she claimed was a humanzee. All that's gone now, of course. Now it's an archive of folklore and local history."

"So?"

"So, if you want to vet my bullshit, sign in at the front desk and tell them you're writing an article or something. Ask for access to old issues of a Spiritualism journal called *Death is the Doorway*. Search for the articles about something called 'The Reternal'. Stella wrote every one of them under a different pseudonym."

They walk on as Graham explains a little more. How Stella mothballed the lumber business and put most of the family land into a conservation easement as a buffer against encroachment. How she hired an empath to serve as some sort of human dowsing rod, and built her manor house among the oldest trees at a spot where the psychic suffered a near-fatal stroke. How she founded some kind of cult-slash-think tank to study this Reternal thing.

"High society spookshow," Graham says. "Private lectures, wacky experiments, lots of séances. Meetings for the morbidly inclined.... Stella never married, but during the Depression she invited a bunch of travelers to camp on the estate and join her new religion."

"Bullshit," Finn says. "What was it called?"

"We don't know," Graham says. "A couple newspaper stories detail a few encounters with the locals, but I've never been able to pin down what they were worshiping or what happened to end it. Stella died not long after that, and her will folded the manor and all the land around into the conservation easement."

By this point they had crested the ridge that hosts the ruins of the manor house. Now fully dark, the risen moon and their adjusted eyes allow them to parse what's left of the building's neo-gothic outlines from the stand of old trees towering behind it. Trees of a size and stature seldom seen anymore, at least not in the east. White pine, oak, eastern hemlock, and sycamore. Massive and silent.

"Holy hell."

Finn fancies himself an urban explorer. He used to hang around after class, helping Graham clean up, and he would talk freely about his crew. They mostly broke into old abandonments, took photographs, got their blood pumping in the dark. That inclination is exactly why he's here. Graham can practically smell his eagerness to spring this dynamite new location on his friends. He decides to let the kid enjoy the thought of it for now.

When Finn darts forward into the clearing, Graham looks at his watch and tells the kid they must wait a little bit.

"Why?"

"We don't want Ed to spot us."

Finn just waits.

"A sort of sentinel," Graham says. "In the sky."

Finn looks up, and then at Graham, searching for the joke.

"He mainly watches over the old frontal road in."

"There's a road?" Finn says. "Why didn't we take the fucking road?"

"I just told you why. About a decade after Stella died, one of her protégés produced a later draft of Stella's will that gave her society claim to the manor. They updated their methods, and the manor briefly housed an institute. The institute built the road."

"Insane asylum?" Finn says,

"No. More like a lab, or an observatory," Graham says.

"For observing what?"

"Officially? Children who couldn't shake their boogeymen."

"Unofficially?" Finn asks.

"How well these troubled kids could communicate with the boogeyman in residence."

"Sorry. I'm not buying it. I've lived here my whole life. How come I never heard any of this?"

"You don't know where 'here' is, remember? You're not even in the same state I picked you up in. In every sense of the word. Besides, the institute only lasted a few years, long before you were born. The lawsuits that shut it down involved powerful individuals on both sides who were strongly motivated to keep it quiet."

The wailing starts as Graham wraps up his prologue. No matter how many times he hears it, the sound never fails to panic him. Not least because it always summons a response from the forest. Finn won't feel it. The senses required only develop after an extended stay or several repeat visits. Cursed with both requisites, Graham is helpless against the effects and far too tweaked to monitor his companion's wellbeing.

As the front edge of it washes over him, he closes his eyes and imagines himself as a sapling wracked by the wind, his limbs puppeteered by a force far stronger and yet more ethereal than anything he can summon to combat it. He uses this relatively benign thoughtform to stop horrible others from gaining a foothold in his mind. A dull razor shaving the unseen side of his face. An electrical jolt sufficient to shit himself. A stiff, queasy yank on the coiled spring of his intestines.

Although he may not hear Ed's wailing or feel the forest throbbing and squirming around him, Finn is still spooked as hell and staring, mouth open, at the giant, creepy head that is peeking over the house and scanning the field with moon-sized eyes. Graham can't look at it any more. To see his old friend's mug so cruelly inflated, eyes about to pop, madcap visage hanging over them like a parade float demon.

"What. The fuck. Is *that?*"

"That's Ed," Graham manages to say. "Or some damned projection of him anyway. When he floats behind the house we have to run like hell."

"Excuse me?" Finn asks, but Graham is already in motion. The search routine is random enough that Graham has never pinned it down to an absolute minimum. His rough guess is five minutes for the sentinel to circle back. In his nimbler years that was plenty of time, but now it is just enough. If and only if he gets his wrinkly ass in gear.

"What happens if it sees us?" Finn shouts from somewhere behind him.

By the time Graham has found the breath to answer him, Finn is bounding ahead in that long stride and skip-hop-correction that younger, nimbler people use to navigate a downhill run. Graham's gait is more like Olympic racewalking done by a sad drunk toeing a tightrope between narrow escape and a DUI.

"Nothing... good," Graham gets out just before he clips an unexpected hump in the terrain and goes down hard. Pain sluices down his back, floods his knees, and squirts across one cheekbone. He tastes debris in his mouth, and the serrated stems of the tall grasses catch and tug on his chapped lips. He has time to think, *What a stupid way to go*, and then he feels Finn's arms under an armpit, trying to lug him up. How touching. Graham doubts he'd still be doing that if he had the slightest clue what they were running towards.

Finn gets Graham up and moving again. They are still only halfway across the field when they both hear the Dopplering wail of Ed's head coming back.

They run for their lives, knowing they will lose, but just before Ed clears his sightline of the house, something impossible happens and they slip into the ineffable.

***

"How did you find this place?" Finn says as their flashlights spirograph across the crumbling walls of a once-grand foyer. Like the moiling of the forest, Finn has not consciously experienced the gap in their timeline. If it ever registers at all, it will be like a spider darting across the windshield of a speeding car. Every time he looks it will be far from where it was before, but he can only assume it must have crawled there. He will not remember Ed's giant head freezing in place and exploding with a wet pop. The staccato slideshow of surrealist visions signaling The Reternal's intervention—night as day, field as glacier, glacier as granite, granite as magma, magma as a dark endless void swallowing creation... and then the whiplash reverse loop of time hurtling back to an approximate present. Clean, intact and ignorant. Finn cannot grasp yet how old Willy Shakes only got it half right. The past is not just prologue but epilogue as well. Outside this loop is where the real magic happens. Those trapped inside are all dumb Calibans to a race of Prosperos beyond their conception.

"Ed found it, not me," is all Graham actually says.

They make their way down what was once the front hall and into the atrium. A rusty iron grid of skylights remains two stories overhead, but the glass is long gone. A coiling vine of sweet autumn clematis has climbed inside, and its flowers look down upon them like curious faces in the dark.

"Ed?" Finn prods. "That fucking thing in the sky?"

Graham struggles with how to respond. Not just where to start but also where to end. "You ever meet somebody and know right away that they are going to fit into your life somehow? Even if you don't particularly like them? Some part of their shape fits some void in your shape and you have no choice but to pair up and hope you get a glimpse of the big picture when the puzzle is finished? Only the puzzle is never finished, the pieces just keep shuffling?"

"No," Finn says. "Can't say that I have."

"I met Ed Shiflett in the fifth grade, but I didn't really get to know him until tenth. We were lab partners in chemistry. He seemed harmless at first. Quiet, awkward, meek. But also somehow mercurial. Conspicuously weird, but not overtly volatile. Chemistry was my kryptonite, and Ed could have taught the class if he wasn't so intent on sabotaging old Selwyn Landry's experiments. Mute in a crowd, but a total motormouth in private—especially when enthused or agitated. Which was, um, all the time. Ocean-sized antiauthoritarian streak, which I shared to an extent I have never cared to psychoanalyze. Most surprising, given his frail, lanky frame, was his internal fearlessness. Ed simply refused to accept risk as a limiting factor. This put him in almost constant danger, but it also seemed to create its own system of physics. Logic, time, even cause and effect always seemed more liquid around him."

Finn demands specifics to these wild claims, so Graham gives him some examples. Like when he provoked a bully into breaking his orbital bone, just to get the other kid expelled and gone from his life for good. How he always placated the chem teacher by coming after school and cleaning up the lab, but only to gain unsupervised access to his store of volatile materials. How he could calm angry dogs just by putting a steady hand near their snapping mouths, or coax a snake from its hiding spot by rubbing his thumb and forefinger together in small, almost erotic circles. But it went far beyond clever manipulations of people and animals. Ed cultivated an incredible tolerance for pain, and recognized virtually no boundaries at all—legal, psychological, or moral. He once told Graham he would consider his life a failure if society didn't try to commit him at least once. To put some teeth into the boast, he taught himself to dislocate a shoulder in case he ever needed to escape a straightjacket. For shits and giggles, he liked to read controversial books out loud in public: *The Anarchist Cookbook*, the Koran, the *Satanic Bible*. He devoured Colin Wilson's history of the occult and cultivated his 'Faculty X' with the cloistered devotion of a mad monk. During his inevitable Crowley phase, he even copped to practicing solo sex magic and transcendental meditation with zero shame or self-consciousness. Hell, he even toyed for a few hours with trepanation. Until his vision blurred from all the blood. Even without the holes, Ed's head sprouted more ideas and obsessions than most grow hairs. By twelve, he'd already built himself a dark room in the crumbling shed behind his ramshackle house. He showed Graham the steps one afternoon, as he developed what he hoped would be the first ever photo of a bird's soul, taken right after it kamikazed into his kitchen window. Neither of them could say for certain whether the hazy white halo around the bluebird's head was evidence of an avian afterlife, or just an artifact of expired film. After that, Ed started insisting that Graham call him Eadweard, after Muybridge, the photographic pioneer and subject of his latest fixation. Other kids picked up on it and wielded the nickname like a whip. Ed's attendance was already dwindling by that point, but soon grew sporadic, and then stopped altogether. Knowing they were friends, a truancy officer tasked Graham with finding out what was wrong. When Graham dropped by Ed's house to check on him, all Ed's lay-about father would say was that his kid was even "crazier than Charlie".

Great Uncle Charlie, as it turns out, was among the cohort of troubled kids treated at the institute. Came out of there even worse, Ed's pop claimed. Never held a job. Always raving about an invisible doomsday beast that hid in the forest.

"Did Ed know his Great Uncle Charlie?" Graham asked the old man.

"Of course he did." Ed's father lifted a hand towards the back of their property, to where Ed's darkroom sat. "Charlie lived for a while in that shack out yonder. Me and Ed looked after 'im as best we could."

Nobody could tell Ed where the institute was—everyone who'd ever been there was long dead—but bits of family lore had him convinced it was somewhere in state, buried deep in the woods.

Ed spent the rest of what should have been his junior year of high school tracing giant overlapping circles across the region. This was back when hitching was normal and whole chunks of America were still empty of people. Camping where the night found you might get you into trouble, but seldom arrested or shot. Ed didn't even try to hide what he was doing when Graham found him buying a bugout bunker's worth of supplies down at the general store. Once or twice Graham even joined him for a day trip, but without Ed's faith in the place's existence Graham quickly grew bored with the snipe hunt. Weeks, and then months, would go by between sightings of his odd friend—but one day, the summer after he should have graduated, Ed showed up at Graham's house in a lather of excitement.

"You found it?" Graham said.

"You won't believe me until you see it for yourself."

***

Graham lets Finn acclimate to the strangeness of the place before he tries to explain any more. Under Stella's direction it was built like an abbey: cruciform, with monastic sleeping quarters extending from one transept and functional rooms from the other. The atrium forms the nave, or long plank of the cross. The space feels wrong and uncomfortable; ill shaped for life but apt for ritual and maniacal focus. By now Finn is almost certainly suffering from an unease he cannot articulate. The feeling that this ruined house, his own body, the world itself is but a bug-smeared transparency laid upon some dark god's overhead projector.

Finn asks why they are safe inside the ruins of the house, and Graham tells him that isn't strictly true. Yes, dodging the Sentinel is a kind of test. Yes, both Ed and Stella managed to convince The Reternal that not every human is an enemy. But that doesn't mean they're safe.

"Oh. Okay."

Finn is still responding to Graham's vagaries as if they are all part of an elaborate prank. A rite of passage or an initiation into some society of aging Odd Fellows. Which they are, of course, but not in the way Finn imagines.

Graham asks him to recount how they got inside.

Finn clams up, stumped. Eventually he pokes the wooly mammoth in the room. "But… what is it, exactly?"

Answering this just isn't possible without visual aids. Even after he showed Graham, Ed had to explain it half a dozen different ways before Graham understood.

Graham starts off the same way Ed did. By saying that long before Muybridge conducted his groundbreaking studies of motion, he was a landscape photographer. That even then he was studying time, but on a much larger scale. And seeing things. Between… within… *inside* of time. Things that other humans couldn't see.

"He suffered a bad head injury in a stagecoach crash," Graham says. "Muybridge, not Ed. Came back from the accident changed. Sullen, paranoid, but given to flashes of genius. It turns out that Muybridge's real legacy wasn't the technological advancements that led to motion pictures. Or his ability to settle that old bet about whether a horse ever has all four hoofs in the air. It was the psychological effect of seeing time manipulated and exposed for what it really was—just another permeable substrate. Einstein was eight years old when Muybridge published *Animal Locomotion.* Consciously or not, this 'Electro-Photographic Investigation of

Connective Phases' seeped into the public consciousness, and changed us forever." Graham savors each word like a twist of black cherry licorice. "Our depth of field deepened, you understand? Our internal lens telescoped from still frames and close-ups to a more omniscient parsing of the continuum."

Finn smiles at Graham like he is crackhead-crazy, so Graham leads him towards the apse of the house and up to the altar, an elevated offset and what was once old Stella's séance room. The whole back wall of this room is a two-story bank of windows gazing into a wide clearing behind the house. The wood casings are intact, but about half of the original windows are missing. The clearing is a semicircular stage, and the arc of the old growth grove functions like a skene or proscenium. *Deus Ex Arboribus.*

On Ed's first visit he found forty-three of the fifty sheets of cathedral glass intact. The idea occurred to him almost immediately. Dictated by some intelligence other than his own. Every autumn following the one he found it, Ed removed a single pane of glass and used it as the medium for the ambrotypes he made of the field and of the thing in the process of returning there.

In the center of the room is a large irregular hole where the rotted floorboards caved beneath the weight of the ultra-large format camera Ed built to make his images. When that section of the floor cracked open, Ed had just finished preparations for another. He was standing in front of the massive apparatus, readying to remove the lens cap, when the floor beneath him crumbled. His fall sheared through a segment of rusty pipe running beneath the floorboards, which tumbled down ahead of him and lodged there in the damp dirt below. Ed managed to grab the hole's edge as he fell. He held on for as long as he could before slipping and impaling himself on the pipe. The pipe punctured his spleen and cored through a section of his stomach, but it also plugged the wound—leaving him alive, but in a state of dire equilibrium.

Ed's uncanny jumbling of cause and effect followed him into that purgatory. Imbalanced during the accident, a carboy of the iodized collodion he used to bind the silver nitrate tipped into the hole on top of him, soaking him completely. Cellulose nitrate, dissolved in ether and ethanol, was initially patented as a surgical dressing. Ed's binding recipe had enough iodine in it to disinfect the wound and hold off sepsis for a few days.

Anchored by the 1800mm lens he stole from the warehouse of an aerial map-making company, Ed's giant camera also fell forward. The camera's flaring trunk and low center of gravity kept it from falling down through the hole and on top of him. Specially designed for strength, both the lens and the thick glass plate survived the fall. The shutter crashed open and stayed that way for the three days it took Ed to die.

The darkness of the basement kept the image from washing out completely during its extra-long exposure. Graham didn't have Ed's skill with the fixing solution, but he salvaged what he could.

The fogging clumps of dust, the crepe lines of unevenly coated collodion, the speckling at the edges, even the oysters of extra silver—all these technical flaws only enhance its dreadful aspect. Ed's thrashing attempts to disimpale himself render his body as a blurry octopod, limbs ghosted and curling unnaturally around the gaping hole of his wound. By comparison, his head stayed remarkably still. The only features in clear focus are his eyes, which reliably document the way he looked in death. Wide and glowing white. Morbidly beatific. Trained forever on a numinous vanishing point he both welcomed and managed to embalm. Looking closer reveals another, more horrifying truth. Subtle anomalies in the reproduction of his face suggest that Ed had already begun to change. As if the collodion that coated his body protected him from earthly infections while serving as a conduit for another kind.

"We had a standing appointment to meet here every twenty-first of October. Ed's birthday… We'd spend a day setting everything up, a second day making and developing the image, and the third inspecting it and discussing what changes manifested. That year other commitments delayed me until late afternoon on the third and final day."

The state of Ed's camera was the first sign of something amiss. At first Graham thought that his lateness had sent his friend into a destructive rage. The smell of Ed's partial evisceration was what eventually led him to the hole.

When he finally managed to dislodge and remove the unwieldy apparatus, a bit of light angled down from the highest windows, shot through the hole, and struck his friend in the pit. The whole scene had the gruesome sublimity of a Caravaggio. Ed look crucified down there. Splayed and pinned like a specimen. Pale to the point of translucency. On closer inspection, Ed coughed to life and sprayed Graham's face with blood. Graham gave him water, but it probably leaked out. He held Ed's hand and gave his word when Ed begged him to finish the work. Had he tried extracting his old friend, he would have only hastened the inevitable. Graham lined the walls of the séance room with the eleven ambrotypes Ed made before he died, along with the twenty-three that Graham subsequently made in his honor. The backs of each are painted with black varnish to make a positive of the negative. Sometimes a simple pun is enough to bring one's purpose into focus.

Ed's snuff selfie is mounted just inside the door, where he can gaze forever at the field and what is forming there. Beside it are a pop-up darkroom, shelves of chemicals, and the giant box camera Graham rebuilt with heavy duty casters to allow for safer positioning.

Finn instinctively shies away from Ed's image, but he does canvass the room, moving like a gallery patron from ambrotype to ambrotype and inspecting them with his flashlight. He appears more curious than disturbed by what they depict. In sequence, the images make it impossible to dispute that something is manifesting in the clearing. At the pace of glaciers and tectonic plates, perhaps, but no less catastrophic. An apt metaphor, Graham supposes, given its apparent size, and the force it seems to wield upon the world around it. In each successive image the giant trees around it perceptibly bow outward. Despite all these hints and rumors, the Reternal's exact form is still elusive; its aspect keeps shifting with each additional parameter. Like a dot-to-dot drawing with not enough numbers yet generated to guess a final shape. What is clear is that the process is quickening. Graham guesses this is why the

Sentinel has become so vigilant—to protect and oversee the final emergence. Five years ago it was just a hurried sketch. Now is has dimension. Rough shading and ragged contours. The suggestion of a central nervous system and various other features in development. Ed seemed able to see it in total, to grasp with zealot clarity both its unearthly aesthetics and the earthly consequence of its arrival. None of this is visible to the naked eye. It is only present on the ambrotypes.

Graham doesn't know why silver nitrate renders it visible. Graham doesn't know if the giant trees serve as antennae to its reception, or somehow summoned it here to save them from a species all too happy to pulp even the most majestic of them for ass wipes and kleenex. Graham doesn't know how the Sentinel works, how it's summoned or controlled, what physics govern it. Graham doesn't know if anyone knows the things he doesn't know, or for that matter the things he does. Graham's one and only certainty is that he doesn't want to come here anymore. He begins his pitch for why Finn should be honored to get the gig. Why, at his age, Graham is no longer fit for this assignment. He promises Finn fame and legend for documenting its arrival. He reminds Finn of something he always said on the first day of class. That in Ancient Greek, the word *ambrotype* translates to *immortal impression*. That should Finn succeed in preserving and presenting this evidence to the world, his name will hang in the firmament with other courageous explorers who advanced our understanding.

Finn finishes his gallery tour and turns around. "What does it want?" he asks.

"I don't know," Graham admits. "Maybe what most visitors want."

"And what's that?"

"To be invited inside," Graham says, "and fed."

Finn lets that sink in before he forces the issue. "What's stopping me from going to the cops?"

"It can sense betrayal. Even in thought. If that's what you're planning... hell, if you even dwell on the *idea* for too long, you won't leave here alive."

"But how can it *do* anything? You said it isn't even here yet."

"I strongly suggest you don't test that hypothesis."

"What happens if I just say no and leave? How am I betraying anything if I never promised it anything?"

Graham hoped that more threats would not be necessary. That he'd chosen someone who might understand. He pulls the Kahr pistol from his waistband holster and points it at Finn's face. With his other hand Graham points down into the hole.

Finn bristles. "Fuck you, man. You actually think you can recruit me by sticking a gun in my face?"

"I'm too old and tired to do this any other way. The only way you leave here alive is to accept my offer and convince us you're sincere."

"What's to stop me from lying to you just to get away?"

"Like I said, it can sense betrayal."

"Then I guess you're fucked then, huh?" Finn says.

The arrogance in Finn's voice is Graham's first indication that he has miscalculated. The second is the crowbar connecting with his skull.

***

When the pain ebbs and again allows for coherent thought, Graham remembers the ambush—but not his fall into the hole. His eyes refocus, and he probes around with his hands to get his bearings. He grimaces when he learns how narrowly he missed the pipe and a gruesome reenactment, but the pain tells him all is definitely not well. His neck and chest are slick with blood. A hematoma grows by the second at the base of his head, just above where it meets his neck. He reaches back and comes away with a blood-soaked hand. The bigger problem is the shard of shinbone poking through a ragged hole in his left pant leg. The pain explodes once he finds its true source. Graham leans over and pukes a little into the dirt. It occurs to him he is seeing things better than he should. He looks up, and within the harsh glare of their flashlights, Graham can see that Finn and someone else are looking down at him.

"Thought ya lost me, didn't ya?" Finn's buddy Petey says. He reaches over, opens Finn's jacket, and retrieves some sort of transmitter from an inner pocket. Beyond the phone, Graham never guessed the kid was bugged.

"You don't understand," Graham croaks. "It might have let you in, but it won't let you leave unless you show it fealty. If you help me out of here I can show you how."

"Fealty?" Petey says. "That's a big word from someone who tried to bail on his invisible monster buddy."

"Typical boomer," Finn says. "Mad hypocritical, yo."

Graham's brain is like his Chevy whenever he gets it stuck in the mud. His wheels just spin and he can't seem to lock the differential. "Wait. You don't understand."

They both laugh. Finn throws down his backpack. "Adios, you crazy fucker," he says. "Good luck with your art project."

Their faces recede from the hole.

The wailing and their eventual screams, the knowledge that the Reternal has some standards after all, provide little comfort throughout that long and painful night.

✳✳✳

Grahams listens to the wind mutter. He watches the light expand and contract through the hole in the floor that is now his ceiling. He thinks of his plight in photographic terms. Point of view, aperture, *camera obscura*. He takes small sips of water from a bottle that never seems to empty. He doesn't die. No, nothing as easy as that. Every attempt at movement results in agony beyond comprehension. He passes out. He comes to. He tries to move again. He passes out once more. He really ought to know better. He isn't going anywhere. Years ago he sealed the only door to this dank basement to keep anyone from disturbing Ed's remains.

✳✳✳

His stomach howls and chews on itself. Over and over again he opens his bag and devours the same stale lump of energy bar he keeps finding inside, but it never dulls the hunger and he never has to shit. Given what he knows already, it takes Graham far too long to understand what is happening. Eventually he drags himself a little closer to Ed's bones and envies them their hard-won equanimity. He lifts Ed's skull, makes Yorick jokes, and cradles this false totem of merciful extinction. Peering into Ed's empty sockets, he pictures his old friend staring out from his glass grave, new-penny eyes still shiny and eager for its arrival.

Every so often, but only for a moment, a willowy shape darts across the hole overhead. Long white hair. Victorian dressing gown on a wiry frame. Her arms stretch wide and reaching, seeking one last dance with some long-lost partner. Graham wants to believe it is Ed who leads Stella in this dance, but in his heart he knows that all three of them have been promised to another.

Black Mariah's Final Form

A dirt road led beyond where the blacktop ended, but Cole saw nothing in need of an address among the acres of soy it bisected. Without the desperate need to be done with this sorry business urging him onward, he would have turned around long before he crested a rise in the terrain and the small, squat homestead revealed itself. When he spotted the old woman sitting out front, the cold stone in his stomach became a brick wrapped in barbwire. After the week he'd just had, he half expected to step from the car and be sprayed with buckshot.

But unlike the others on his list, Mrs. Tilly Perkins did not scream, or curse, or rush forward to rake her nails across his face. Instead she asked him to sit. At least, Cole assumed that's what she conveyed with her blunt wave at the other metal rocker on her concrete porch. There was no sign of deference or hospitality in the gesture, though, just a stiff invitation to get this over with, whatever this might be. Cole waited a moment beside the car for some sort of secondary confirmation, but her eyes never left the fields behind him. Not even as he passed in front of her to take the seat. Wondering what it was she watched out there, he sat and mirrored her gaze a minute before speaking. Every so often a slight breeze would ripple through the soy like the flexing segment of something monstrous moving just beneath the surface of the earth.

"Pretty piece of property you have here, ma'am."

"Fields ain't mine anymore. Reckon I'll need to find better facilities soon."

He assumed she meant an old folks home, but shied away from any sort of follow-up. Best not to get too personal. Instead he asked her if she knew who he was and why he was there. She nodded. Did she remember speaking with him on the phone? She nodded again, still not looking at him. She might not be fixing to attack him, but she wasn't going to make this easy.

Without much else to say, Cole waded in with what he had rehearsed. He reiterated the experimental nature of the project, using language that was a bit more explicit than what was in the written agreement. He reminded her about the liability waivers her grandson had signed. He did not cite the Supreme Court's latest position on felon volunteers, but he had key sections of the majority opinion memorized in case he needed them. He salted his speech with a proper dash of sympathy, but not so much as to sound guilty of anything but attempting to advance the scientific interests of humanity.

The sun continued to sink, but the air refused to give up any of its heat. By the time he'd bullied through his spiel, sweat was streaming down his face and turning the upper half of his white-collared shirt a nearly translucent gray.

By contrast, Mrs. Perkins' neck remained dry. So dry that Cole found himself wondering whether she suffered from some kind of dysplasia that prevented her pores from functioning properly. Spongy skin tags sprouted here and there among the fine gray curls of her remaining hair, and for a surreal moment he entertained the notion that they had soaked up the missing moisture and any moment now would blossom with strange and hostile flowers.

Bodies bothered Cole. Always had, and now more than ever. Every body, really. Even, sometimes especially, his own. Their paradoxical density and squishiness. The sloppy disconnect between a finite sack of flesh and its immeasurable consciousness.

The zombie hordes of autonomous subsystems that allegedly piled up to a self.

Atop this ambient phobic thrum ticked an egg timer of dread. Despite her outward calm, Cole couldn't help but feel that any second now Mrs. Perkins was going to unleash on him. So far the old woman had not even once turned her face in his direction to register the horrible news or the calculated callousness with which he was delivering it. Her silence should have made things easier. A sight better than the righteous hatred and sudden violence he'd suffered earlier that week. But something about her stoic bearing was triggering defense mechanisms he could hardly identify, much less disarm. As if she knew all that he could tell her. Far more, in fact. As if she were simply waiting for him to catch up.

Just before he summoned the words to beg off, Cole heard a sort of moaning sound from inside the house. He had seen no one else about, and assumed she lived alone. The sound was oddly harmonic in its voicing: doubled, yet distinctly individual, with a slight delay in between. Cole swiveled his head to the nearest window but he could see nothing through the overlapping pair of timeworn curtains. Even when they jerked ever so slightly away from the screen, as if tugged by an unseen hand. The twin layers of meshing, the interior gloom, and the contrasting light outside gave Cole the disorienting sensation of descending through layers of skin with a microscope. Distracted and tense as he was, he nearly seized when Mrs. Perkins began to sing.

"Way out west, they got a name, for rain and wind and fire."

She wasn't belting it, by any means. Her voice was both kinds of low.

"The rain is Tess, the fire's Joe, they call the wind Mariah."

Hearing those lyrics sung outside the lab confirmed Cole's sense that he was operating at an informational disadvantage. Black Mariah was the project's internal codename. Singing 'They Call the Wind Mariah' from *Paint Your Wagon* was just a grim, contagious joke, something the techs did to break the monotony. They never meant it to be cruel.

"Why they call it Black Mariah?" Mrs. Perkins said.

"Pardon me?"

"You heard me. Do they only use it on us black folk?"

"Who told you that?"

"Answer my question!"

In the tense lull that followed, that strange moan returned. This time Cole thought he heard within its weird harmony the whimper of a child. As far as he was concerned, kids were the worst kind of bodies. Kids were chaos incarnate.

"Is there a child in there? Do you need to—" he said.

"Never mind her," she cut in. "Gets fussy this time of day is all. Answer the question."

At first Cole thought maybe she made her money looking after other people's children. The idea of it overwhelmed him for a second. Then a detail from the skimmed case file sitting on his passenger seat floated over in the hot, still air.

Marcus had a daughter.

When invited to volunteer for their experiments, Mrs. Perkins's grandson had just started serving a life sentence for murdering a liquor store owner killed during a robbery. Marcus pled not guilty, and claimed throughout the trial that he was the wrong man, at home looking after his baby daughter at the time. He had a couple arrests for pot possession and disturbing the peace. Nothing violent, just stupid stuff from his youth, but none of it helped. An oddly confident identification by the wife hiding in the back carried more weight with the jury than an alibi from an infant. The file said nothing about the child's mother or Marcus's parents, but presumably Great Grandma Perkins played a role in raising her.

"It's complicated," Cole said, shifting in his seat. He was pretending to get more comfortable, but what he was really doing was angling away from the window so that he might at least avoid an ambush. The thought of this child's hand tugging at his neck like it had with the curtain was giving him the screaming meemies.

"How 'bout you uncomplicate it then?" Mrs. Perkins said. "You owe me that much. And you can start by leaving out the fifty-cent words. You ain't impressing anybody."

She was right of course. He owed her that much, and more. But fifty-cent words were where he banked all his social anxiety. Long before the Asperger's diagnosis or the hard-won PhD, ever since he could read on his own really, they'd been pouring out of him like a slot machine stuck on jackpot.

"It originated with a racehorse," Cole said. "Born in Harlem, 1826. Some sources run wild with this, no pun intended, and claim a connection between *Mariah* and *Mare*, which is interesting given the implicit connection to *nightmare....*"

Mrs. Perkins found that neither implicit nor interesting. Her face screwed up at his robot-librarian routine.

"Other sources say it started as colorful vernacular for a marooned ship, or a horse-drawn hearse. Dreaded vessels of death. That sort of thing. It seems to have become a catchall for any large black mode of transport. By 1846, it was mainly used as a synonym for police escort vehicles. You know, paddywagons. James Joyce used it that way in *Ulysses*. There are cognates with that meaning in Dutch, Swedish, Russian, Finnish, almost certainly other languages as well."

Wordy as all that was, it was still only half the story. He left out the Black Mariah variants of hearts and stud poker, despite a deep fascination with the meta relevance of a wild card that gets reassigned every time the Queen of Spades appears. For all sorts of obvious reasons, he wasn't comfortable sharing the probably-apocryphal-anyway explanation from Brewer's 1898 *Dictionary of Phrase and Fable* that traces the term to a Black rooming house owner in Boston by the name of Mariah Lee—a woman as infamous for her great bulk as for her habit of snitching on johns who abused her girls. He skipped as well the Marvel comic book villain modeled after her, enemy to Luke Cage and memorably portrayed by Alfre Woodard in the TV series. In the interests of time, Cole also left out the term's use by Scottish soldiers in WWI as slang for the sixteen-inch shells fired by the largest German artillery, which Cole assumed traced back to its meaning of a transport for death. He likewise neglected the series of experimental diesel-electric locomotives, which almost certainly referred back to the racehorse.

"Black Mariah was also the nickname of Thomas Edison's experimental film studio," Cole went on. "The first to use special effects, by the way, when they recreated the beheading of Mary, Queen of Scots. No special effects needed in 1903, though, when they filmed the first legally sanctioned electrocution. A Coney Island fixture named Topsy the Elephant was executed for the crime of killing one of its trainers. It's this intersection of prisoner transport and pioneering technology where our team's use of it begins to make sense."

"Not to me it don't," Mrs. Perkins said.

"I'm sorry, ma'am. I'm a real motormouth when I get going. What do you need me to clarify?"

"I don't need anything from you but the truth."

"Our Black Mariah was an experimental engine of teleportation," he said. "Do you know what teleportation means?"

"I'm not stupid, junior," she said. "I've seen Star Trek."

"Well, I led the team that made it work in real life."

Cole didn't suppress the pride in his voice. Even now, even here, even to her, he could separate the technical feat from its awful application.

"You made it work, huh? How's that?"

"Basically, we turned matter into data by passing it through a small, artificial black hole."

She wrinkled her nose at the thought of it.

"As momentous as that was, though, that turned out to be the easy part. The real trick was how to retrieve the data and turn it back into matter. Explaining how we did that would fill a whole high school's worth of blackboards with equations you wouldn't understand. Suffice it to say that we ultimately used quantum entanglement to dodge the whole problem. We shaped the event horizon in such a way that the test subject was both entering and exiting the black hole at the same instant.

"Inanimate objects were pretty straightforward. Scrape a sample for the post-port checksum, scan it, encode it, check for consistency, and bam! Bob's your uncle. We got all sorts of things to pop into the decom chamber, just like that tennis ball in

Poltergeist. Living things… well, living things weren't quite that simple. The problem was not just what we were teleporting, but when. The atoms in living things are never static, right? They're superfast curveballs of organic entropy. Can't hit a curveball if you lose sight of it, even for an instant. Might as well close your eyes. But once we were able to clock our cell state capture to within a few thousandths of a second, we could lock in the when, more or less. Any organism could then be expressed in a finite amount of code. But the file size for a human being… well, it was just astronomically huge, and the quantum packets we use for transport can only hold so much data—"

"The what now?"

"People were basically too… ample to fit through our tiny black hole."

"Hmm," Mrs. Perkins said, disappointed. "But my Marcus was lean."

"Yeah, well, I didn't mean it literally. Anyway, we solved that problem too. Back in 2018 biologists announced the discovery of a new organ."

Mrs. Perkins exhaled through her nose hard enough to clear both nostrils. "Can't you do this any faster?"

"I'm sorry, ma'am, but if you want a real explanation, I'm afraid this is as fast as I can go."

She just stared into space and waited, and so he went on.

"They called it the 'interstitium'. You know how if you look up into the sky at night there's all this space between the stars? Well, the interstitium is our inner space. A layer of fluid padding in our organs. Inside our skin, inside our blood. Quite large in proportion. A whole lot of relatively empty inner space. The key thing to understand is that it's more or less the same in everyone. Just water and collagen. The interstitium gave us a new constant for a much more radical compression algorithm." He paused again, looking to see if he'd lost her, but Mrs. Perkins was right behind him.

"You fried out all the fat and crammed the cracklins through the hole."

"Exactly!"

"Then you tried adding it back on the other side. With a computer or something. Like my Marcus was a cup of instant you could toss in a microwave."

"Yes! Exactly. Instant being the operative word. At least in theory. In the same way the human ear cannot tell the difference between a properly encoded MP3 file and its original, full-spectrum recording, our teleported subjects should have been, well, for all intents and purposes, they should have been the same. Moreover, if we did our job properly, the entire process should be imperceptible to the subject."

"But you *didn't* do your job properly!" And she started singing again before he could protest. Slow and low, same as before. Each word ripping up something rooted way down deep. *"Mariah blows the stars around. And sends the clouds a-flying. Mariah makes the mountain sound like folks were up there dying."*

Cole did his best to hide how much that verse disturbed him. When she trailed off again, he tried to explain. "It did take us a while to finetune it, and yes, we did make a lot of... well, nothing to call them but mistakes, but by early last year we had successfully teleported seven worms, three frogs, two kittens, and a puppy."

"No chimps?" Mrs. Perkins asked.

"Our CEO has strict prohibitions against experimenting on animals of a certain order."

"No problem with convicts though, huh?"

"No, ma'am. So long as they can consciously consent."

"Hmm. I reckon once you dangle a little pardon ain't hardly a one who don't consent?"

"Hardly a one," Cole agreed.

"But if you knew it would work, you wouldn't need to offer pardons!"

Cole winced. "Would it make you feel any better if I told you I was the one who blew the whistle? They fired me for it too. Probably tanked my career. They even threatened my parents to keep my mouth shut. Despite all that, I'm out here of my own volition, telling you the truth."

"None of that makes a lick of difference to me."

"Then I don't know what else I can do."

"I do. You can tell me what happened to my grandson."

This time he was ready for her singing. At least he thought he was. Until she got to the end and his mind shrank from the image it made in his head.

"Then one day I left my girl. I left her far behind me. And now I'm lost, I'm oh so lost not even God can find me."

"The truth is we don't know," Cole said after a long silence, hoping she would finally hear the regret in his voice. Hoping he could leave it at that. But her face made it abundantly clear he could not. Something had changed in the composition of the scene, and Cole felt compelled to determine what.

Formerly turned away, or shrouded in late afternoon shadow, her face was now lit with a strange glow. Almost like a Renaissance painting of a martyred saint, only one done by Kehinde Wiley. Cole blinked a few times, his sense of reality abandoning him until he realized that the sun had dipped enough to trigger the solar cell of her porch light. He took a breath. Opened his mouth. Closed it. Opened it again, and began to tell her the full truth. "I'm no longer convinced that teleporting a human being will ever be possible. Especially when the human in question is a prisoner. At first we had no idea what was going on. We'd put the subject in the compression chamber—"

"What happens to the original?" Mrs. Perkins said.

"Pardon?" Cole said.

"Do they go through the black hole or not?"

"It doesn't make sense on anything but the quantum level. We collected the one that didn't, just before it did."

"You just made a Xerox machine! That ain't teleporting."

"Well, the distinction is fine enough to be numerically irrelevant. We captured and transported complex biostates in their entirety, ma'am. Mid-heartbeat. Mid firing of synapses. That puppy I mentioned? It teleported while scratching an ear and continued scratching on the other side!" He left out the fact that it never stopped scratching. Not until it hit brain matter.

"I'm gonna ask you again. What happened to my Marcus?"

"I'm not sure that's a healthy thing to focus on."

"Why can't you people ever give a straight answer?"

"The antecedents are annihilated. Is that what you wanted to hear?"

The look she gave Cole then was not one he could withstand. He dropped his eyes before going on.

"As I was saying, imprisoned humans delivered results that were entirely unpredictable. Sometimes… um, well, sometimes a *portion* of the subject would come through and we'd think something went wrong with the decompression algorithm. Until we found the other portions… elsewhere. Embedded in the prison wall. Grafted with a particular tree just beyond the fence line. In one case some remains were recovered from the trunk of a car that happened to be driving by the prison at the time of the experiment. We thought the data packets were splintering and energy was leaking somewhere. We thought information might have gotten lost in the black hole. But we could measure it exiting. Nothing was lost. We just couldn't direct or contain it. Eventually we reasoned it had something to do with desire."

"Desire?" She said it like the thing expressed by the word existed at a great distance from her, something dimly remembered. Or maybe she said it like that thing was far too close and precious to acknowledge at all, lest it drive her mad.

"Whatever you want to call it," Cole said. "Faith. Willpower. Intention. The quantum soul. Shed of mass, if only for nanoseconds, the information that comprises a fully sentient being refused to behave in predictable ways. Or, more accurately, in controllable ways. Despite our every attempt to corral them, they broke out and followed their own prime directive. Which in the case of the prisoners meant escape. Most of them didn't get very far. None that we know of did so intact. A very small number eluded our recovery teams and disappeared altogether. Your grandson Marcus was one of those. I like to believe he won his freedom. That he's out there somewhere, living a new life… but that's just wishful thinking."

Mrs. Perkins was shaking her head and stroking her bottom lip. So hard Cole worried she might rub away some skin. She'd turned away from him again. Beyond her the fireflies had begun to wink in and out of sight.

"How many people you try this on before you shut it down?" she asked the dark.

There seemed no point in hiding anything else, given what he'd already shared.

"Twenty-two," Cole admitted. "Twenty-seven if you count the cadavers."

"How many were people of color?"

"Too many," Cole said quickly. "Ma'am, that's why I'm here. To do my penance. What can I say besides I am utterly and terribly sorry?"

"Ain't enough. Not even by your reckoning. You need to meet someone before you go." Mrs. Perkins finished her song for good measure. If before her tone was barbed, now it was just bone-weary and blue. *"Out here they got a name for rain. For wind and fire only. But when you're lost and all alone, there ain't no word but lonely."*

By then it was country dark and Cole felt on the verge of collapse. He'd been out on the road delivering terrible news for the better part of two weeks. He had one hell of a rough drive ahead of him to get back to his hotel room. The last thing on earth he wanted to do was meet the child of someone he killed.

"I'm sorry, ma'am, but I really need to get going."

"Uh-uh. No way. Not yet. All this time you've been dancing round your devilry, using fancy words and fancy ideas to keep from feeling anything. Trying to quiet them screams in your head. Time to lose them words and listen, son. Time to sit with what you done."

They didn't enter the house through the front. Instead they went around to a side door. Mrs. Perkins insisted that he walk out ahead of her. She didn't help him find his way by turning on any additional lights. Once off the porch, Cole had to put his hands out in front of him to keep from colliding with anything.

"Sure gets dark out here," he said.

"Just you wait," Mrs. Perkins said.

Lone trees and other unidentifiable clusters of denser dark in the foreground gave him the impression of an audience, of some sort of shadow gallery assembled in mute witness of a gallows walk. Eventually he found the screen door he was supposed to enter, but its spring was shot, or gone entirely, and he nearly fell over at its lack of resistance, his weight working against him, a desperate grip on the handle the only thing keeping him upright. It was hardly any less dark inside. Low ceilings and a clutter of old furniture enhanced the feeling of walking into a trap. A few circular nightlights at each outlet led him into the living room; dim orange moons hovering like small faces just above the baseboards.

Mrs. Perkins finally cut on a small lamp in the entranceway, just as Cole was turning around to ask her who it was she wanted him to meet.

She just jabbed her chin in the opposite direction.

For a second he felt as if he'd placed himself into the Black Mariah. Space and reality were bending out of shape. The small living room had been converted into a makeshift nursery. A rickety plywood base supported a freestanding wash basin. Even in that meager light he could see the water was tinted red with blood. Piles of towels and extra sheets were neatly folded beside it. Dominating the room, and blocking the front door, was a second-hand hospital bed. On the bed, coiled and flexing, was a tangle of limbs that took a few seconds to mentally unravel. When the shock subsided a little, Cole understood that he was looking at the meshed bodies of Marcus Perkins and his daughter.

The fusing was thorough. Seemingly haphazard and yet somehow viable. Angry welts marked every visible point of intersection. Skin upthrust along the fault lies, already knitting into scar tissue. Overlapping tendons strained and bulged. The child thrashed within her second womb. Marcus flailed his misplaced arms in a vain attempt to cradle her.

When they lifted their heads and looked at him, Cole saw how nearly their hearts overlapped. How closely their movements synced. His eyes jerked away and his mind threatened to flee the scene entirely, but he forced himself to look back. As their mouths opened in furious overtone, Cole did as he was told.

He sat with what he had done. He lost his words and listened.

They spoke of old evils with ever-evolving definitions. Of jails and hearts and hearses. Of power, projection, and invention. Vessels of doom and instruments of war. A dread carriage of justice and revenge. They even named the driver.

When they finished speaking, Cole's eyes were shining with shame and awe. Their plan was masterful; audacious and genius enough to outdo Edison. Cole only nodded once. Both to confirm that it was possible, and to confirm that he was willing to execute it. Behind him, in a lullaby whisper, Mrs. Perkins resumed her song.

"Mariah blows the stars around. And sends the clouds a-flying. Mariah makes the mountain sound like folks were up there dying."

THE ANA LOG

I think I found her. Phone call today from Bob Thornbill, a fellow collector here in Richmond. We had a long-standing agreement for me to be first in line should he ever locate the tapes, and now he is not only claiming to know where they are—but to actually have them in his possession. More importantly, he expressed a strong desire to sell them. He did not waste words or ask an impossible price. We made plans to meet at his shop on Saturday. I can hardly believe this is happening. Nearly two decades of searching, and she is finally within my reach.

***

Besides the crime scene in the basement, Burke's diary is the only hard evidence left, and in a little while I am going to burn that too. Whatever she is, she deserves to rest in peace, not be further desecrated. But the archivist in me refuses to erase her completely, so before I do, I am going to transcribe a few entries here together with enough supplementary information to tell the whole story. I am confident that I can document her case online without invoking the iterative damnation those devils designed for her. I cannot be certain, of course, but the lack of any fallout from all that Usenet activity in the early '90s suggests that a physical record or transducer of some sort is necessary to trigger her recursive properties, so when I am finished she should remain deactivated, as it were, as long as these words are never printed, published or otherwise reproduced in anything but the digital domain.

SATURDAY, FEBRUARY 5

Nondescript and nearly swallowed by the general blight of Jefferson Davis Highway, Thornbill's store gives no clue that it houses the largest extant VHS collection on the East Coast. And that's just what's on the shelves, available for rent to anyone willing to pay the $5 membership fee.

He locked his front door, turned his sign to Closed, and escorted me down an impressive gauntlet of vintage porn, through a steel door and into a vast, climate-controlled storeroom in the back that housed a large quantity of unknowns. I was tempted to inquire about certain other rarities that had long eluded me, but in the end felt it best to focus on the task at hand.

Inside a framed and sheet-rocked subdivision of the storeroom, Thornbill had a HR-S8000U *hooked up to a Sony Triniton CRT. The inner walls of this room were lined with soundproofing tiles to allow for the private screening of any manner of material. Thornbill excused himself for a moment and returned with an aluminum attaché case, which he placed on the table, unlocked, and then opened. It contained eight VHS-C cassettes of the make and vintage I was expecting, plus a folder full of photos and police reports.*

Thornbill powered on the VCR and the television, presented me with an adapter cassette, and then excused himself again. As he left the room, I asked if he had seen the tapes. He said he had not, and would like to keep it that way—but he had every confidence that they were genuine. He had acquired them directly from a retired Richmond P.D. captain. Thornbill said this in a way that made it clear from which direction my troubles would come if I were ever foolish enough to be indiscreet with this information. I asked him why his source had decided to sell them now, after all these years. Thornbill said the man had protected her for as long as he could, and just needed someone else to shoulder the burden.

It was a strange choice of words, overly metaphoric for a cop. I was eager to take possession of the tapes and be gone with them before Thornbill changed his mind, but I also wanted to be certain the material was genuine. I inserted the first five tapes, in sequence, and watched a few minutes of each. I knew almost immediately that things would never be the same.

***

A fair amount of backstory is necessary to understand Burke's excitement. The facts are these: In 1985, George Veitch was a freshman at Virginia Commonwealth University, planning to major in film and photography. Like many young men, Veitch became fixated on a girl; a girl he called Ana. Among a cohort of neon personalities and outsized egos, Veitch evidently noticed the thin pale thing with the cornsilk hair precisely *because* she tried very hard to disappear.

According to his signed statement, Veitch first noticed her at a cafeteria, sitting alone and staring at her food, and then again when they both entered James Branch Cabell Library at the same time. He followed her to the third-floor stacks and spied on her as she collected a pile of books and sat down to speedread them. He watched her do this for two hours without pause before he had to go to class. After that, Veitch sort of haphazardly stalked her from afar for several weeks, but did not actually meet her face to face until their paths crossed by chance one night at Hollywood Cemetery, back when you could still go there at night without getting thrown in jail for it.

As part of his college send-off, Veitch's parents had bought him a JVC GR-C1, one of the first VHS-C camcorders on the consumer market. It was a lavish gift and a coveted item among budding filmmakers, especially after its cameo in *Back to the Future*. This particular video camera had a big splash of oxblood red on its body, so different from the army of conformist blacks and grays that followed, and with the right personality its ownership would have conferred on Veitch an instant posse (as perhaps his parents had hoped)—but he was too odd and antisocial, even for an art school crowd, and instead of luring in companions it became another reason he had none. Subsequent police interviews with a few of his peers insinuated that he was seldom seen in public without the thing perched on his shoulder, obscuring half his face, and whenever he passed by a joke was inevitably made at his expense.

Whatever the case, he had the camera with him that night at the cemetery. We know this because Tape #1 starts off with a succession of moonlit trees and tombstones. These establishing shots, though amateurish, provide an oddly fitting prologue to everything that follows. After twenty minutes of aimless wandering, Veitch happens upon Ana doing a charcoal sketch of the cast iron dog that guards the grave of a young scarlet fever victim. Until that point, Veitch's breathing is clearly audible through the camera's mic—especially as he ascends a rise in the terrain—but when he sees Ana, his breath catches in his throat. Its sudden absence betrays the shock he feels at finding her there, alone and engaged in some secret activity. Ana is so absorbed in her drawing that Veitch is able to approach and film her for nearly ten minutes before she notices him. Her sketch pad is laid out on the ground and she is kneeling in front of it, sitting on her heels. She has an unsettling way of rocking back and forth while she works that makes her look like a medium in full trance. The impression is only deepened by the way she periodically prostrates herself and attacks the canvas with the charcoal. She is rocking like that—a flaxen metronome beneath a full moon—when she finally detects Veitch's presence behind her. Any normal girl would have screamed or fled or lashed out in anger, but Ana merely turns her head in the slow, steady fashion of a Victorian automaton. Her face is pale, oval, and betrays no recognizable emotion. Her large brown eyes are more like mirrors than windows to a soul. Tape #1 ends with this first haunting close up, and anyone unlucky enough to see it is condemned never to forget it.

It is difficult to believe that this encounter provoked a relationship—even one as unusual as theirs—but in the ensuing weeks Veitch not only made Ana's acquaintance, he somehow convinced her to sit for six separate interviews comprising nearly four hours of footage. The project got off to a very strange start, and it only got stranger from there. The entire first hour depicts Ana doing nothing but peering dolefully into the camera as if she is trying to wordlessly communicate with an unknown audience. The blanks Veitch recorded his footage on only held thirty minutes each, so that means two entire tapes of nothing but a stare contest between Ana and the camera. Someone with less abundant parental support might have been inclined to save tape and stop recording, but in addition to nonexistent interview skills, Veitch evidently had unlimited patience and funds to spend on blanks. He kept the camera rolling throughout these thirty-minute segments of unnerving silence.

Veitch stays off camera and says nothing throughout Tapes #2 and #3, but shortly into Tape #4 he finally begins prodding Ana with questions, and occasionally she answers them. Asked to recall a special moment from her past, she thinks a while and describes a fairly generic day at the beach. Veitch presses her for more details, and she talks about a starfish she found stranded by the tide; how strange it was, and how lovely. She put it back into the water but it was long dead and just floated on the surface, casting a shadow of itself onto the ocean floor. Veitch doesn't know what to do with this information, so he changes the subject and asks about her parents. Ana doesn't want to talk about them. Veitch asks how she pays for her rent or tuition, and she doesn't seem to understand the question. Veitch then asks where she is from. At this point, Ana begins her metronome routine.

Later police inquiries with the Student Accounting Office at VCU revealed that no one named Ana fitting her description was ever enrolled at the university, and any classes she might have taken must have been surreptitiously attended. A call to her landlord only deepened the mystery. As far as he knew, her unit was vacant.

During the entirety of her testimony, Ana's voice remains disturbingly calm, never rising above a monotone. The frame is usually tight on her face, but occasionally zooms out to reveal that she is surrounded by hundreds of charcoal drawings that have been affixed to every square inch of her apartment without apparent rhyme or reason. Most of them have a photorealistic quality, capturing everything an average person might see in his or her daily life: trees, people, buildings, vehicles, animals, food, furniture. Nothing is too trivial, yet no scene or subject is duplicated, bar one. Scattered in amongst all the others is a large quantity of drawings that depict a small, solitary, semi-human figure cowering beneath the gaze of something that lies beyond the borders of the image. At one point, midway through Tape # 5, Veitch asks her why she feels compelled to sketch this one scene over and over. Ana stops rocking and says nothing for what feels like an eternity before answering.

"Because they are always watching."

Veitch gives her answer some air before he responds. "Who is always watching?"

Ana begins to answer, and then something stops her.

Once witnessed, what happens next cannot be forgotten, and yet is impossible to describe. It simply must be seen to be appreciated and, unfortunately, for reasons which will soon become clear, I have already destroyed the tapes. So I can present no hard evidence. You have nothing but my word to go on, and I am the direct cause for this. So be it. You will either believe me or you won't. In time I suspect you will have no choice.

At first Ana appears to return to whatever fugue state she entered in Tapes #2 and #3. She stares at the camera, unblinking, for two minutes and thirteen seconds. At the 18:52 mark, she glitches. It happens again at 18:59, seven seconds later. The background image stays solid. A lamp by her right elbow, the drawings hung behind her, the arms of the chair she is sitting in… all remain distinct and unchanged. Only Ana's face and upper body grotesquely distort, smear to the right and, for the briefest of moments, disappear completely. The second instance is similar, with the exception that just before it happens Ana senses it coming. Her mouth opens, she again attempts to answer, and then her jaw slides to the left while the rest of her face blurs to the right. There is another split-second subtraction of her body... and then she's back, and reset to default.

Digital video effects and anomalies come in many different forms, and nowadays are easily faked. Just about anything you can dream up can be fairly convincingly created. But analog video is a different animal altogether. I have been in this business for nearly forty years, and have seen every trick in the book. Burke was even more versed than I. It is patently impossible to create such an effect on the fly. The tapes were timestamped and clean. They displayed no physical doctoring.

Veitch reacts immediately and violently. He can clearly be heard crying out and falling backwards, or otherwise scrambling from an overturned chair. For her part, Ana appears to sense that something has happened, but doesn't seem to grasp its importance. Not right away. She looks distracted by what activated the glitch. She is still trying to answer the question. While Veitch is making sounds of continued shock and alarm in the background, Ana leans in and tries to voice box the words through clenched teeth, but all that comes out is an emphatic hiss.

TUESDAY FEBRUARY 8

Three days of nothing but viewing the tapes, several times each. No doubts about their authenticity. Part of me now wants to turn them over to the authorities. Not the Richmond P.D., of course—who clearly had no understanding of what this case was all about—but an agency much higher up the food chain. The better, saner part of me knows with absolute certainty what will happen if I do: nothing at all. Nothing to see here. Move along.

Instead I will stay the course. I've made contact with at least two potential buyers, one abroad and one here in the States. The money I am asking ensures that these individuals or the organizations they represent have the resources and the wherewithal to actually do something about this. What that might be, I cannot say. I am just a middleman, like Thornbill. The only difference is that I have seen the tapes, so I know the true value of what I possess.

***

Veitch stopped the camera when he recovered his footing, so we can't know what happened next or how he came to grips with what he had seen and been told, but whatever dismay he felt was overridden by his incessant need to document. Tape #6 is Veitch filming Ana's reaction to Tape #5.

When inserted into an adapter cassette, VHS-C tapes are playable in a normal VCR. Ana must not have owned one, because the scene changes to Veitch's tiny dorm room. His desk is almost entirely obscured by a large tube TV, a VCR, and a coiled pile of assorted cables. Ana's face is awash in cathode glow. Veitch films her over her shoulder, at a wide enough angle to capture a bit of both Anas.

At first glimpse of herself, Ana's face clouds over and she begins to rock. "Is that me?" she asks.

It is a strange question. To me it suggests that she was on the cusp of understanding what she really was.

Veitch doesn't answer, choosing with his characteristic detachment to play the silent observer. Ana leans in and watches with greater intensity. When the first glitch occurs onscreen, she stops rocking. The second glitch drives a lightning rod straight down her spine and applies high voltage. The chair topples backward and Ana's head hits the tiles with a series of sickening thuds. The seizure lasts a minute and eight seconds, and during it the glitches come fast and furious, contorting Ana's body into impossible postures. Veitch doesn't try to restrain her or help in any way. He only films.

Friday, February 11

Unanticipated developments. Both potential buyers backed out without saying why. More troubling, I may have seen Ana. Earlier tonight I got some air and a bite to eat and when I glanced out the large windows at the front of the restaurant, I saw a dead ringer staring back at me with her face pressed against the glass.

Whoever it was, she was gone by the time I could get out there to check. I know what happened to Veitch. But I also know that there are lots of thin pale girls with long blonde hair and big brown eyes in this world, and at this point I am choosing to assume it was simply a look-alike.

***

According to the time stamps, six days elapsed between the date of the seizure and the beginning of Tape #7. According to Veitch's statement, Ana cut off contact for nearly a week and then, with no fanfare or drama, came to his dorm room one day and asked him to assist in her suicide. That he was not only willing to do so, but also interested in filming it, says quite a bit about this young man. Either he understood with preternatural calm that he was not dealing with a human being, or he was a closet sociopath. He certainly gave no thought to consequences, or he would have suggested some other location than the girls' showers on the second floor of his own dorm.

Perhaps he was expecting her to vaporize like a lightbulb filament, or fade away in a puff of green smoke like a Sleestak from *Land of the Lost.* Instead he got a gruesome, thirty-minute death scene that stays close on Ana long after she is dead, and is only broken when a pair of female students enter the bathroom together and find Veitch passed out on the floor. They don't stick around long enough to discover what he was filming in the shower stall.

Ana slits her wrists the wrong way, as if she learned how to do it from a movie, and sits down on the shower floor and waits for death with the same haunted stare she trained on life. When it takes too long, she lifts the razor again and slits her own throat.

Veitch had bothered to set up a tripod, and so the shot stays straight and true even after he faints. Right up until the camera runs out of tape.

She stayed a Jane Doe in the press for the ten days her story garnered any attention. When asked who she was, Veitch was forced to admit he didn't know. He had come up with the nickname "Ana" as a cutesy diminutive of "anonymous" while labeling the first tape. He got so used to calling her Ana he stopped wondering what her real name might be. In any case, no one came forward to claim her or identify the body, and interest faded fast without any new information. Police searched Veitch's dorm room and found the other tapes, but because the footage clearly showed Ana killing herself, he was not held or charged with any crime. The police returned his camera but kept the tapes, putting them in a box with his statement and the statements obtained from the two female witnesses, the VCU Accounting Office, the landlord of the building Ana was squatting in, and several other students interviewed by police. A few remembered seeing someone fitting her description on campus, but none had ever spoken to her. If any police watched the other tapes, they stayed quiet about it, even after Veitch was found floating in the James River. His coroner's report went into the case box as well. It ruled his death a suicide by drowning, and suggests the damage to his eyes was done post mortem, by animals feeding on his remains. But Veitch was only in the water for a few hours.

MONDAY, FEBRUARY 14

Still no buyer so I have decided to go public with the tapes. I don't trust the YouTube generation to make anything but a freakish mockery of her, so I must rely on the traditional media. May not make me any money, but at least the truth will get out. I'm hoping the attention earns me some protection as well. I can no longer ignore the fact that Ana, or something just like her, has followed me home.

I've seen her lurking in the stand of trees across the street, and lingering in the yard, staring up at my house. It is her. Of course it's her. And yet not her: a degraded copy. The skin tone is all wrong and her face is out of whack.

It is hard to tell if she is just keeping tabs on me, or asking for my help.

***

Veitch's body was found ten days after Ana tried to kill herself. I say "tried" because although Tape #7 graphically depicts her death, Tape #8 makes it just as clear that she failed to stay dead. Police found the final tape in Veitch's dorm room, still inside the camcorder. As with the others, they confiscated the evidence and put it in the case box, but released the video camera to Veitch's parents. I wonder whether they knew their fancy gift was the engine of his demise.

Veitch captured her image nearly a dozen more times. Most are very brief glimpses of her flitting around campus or Hollywood Cemetery, but the worst of them shows her standing outside Veitch's ground-floor room, staring in through the window. The light is low and the crosshatching of the window screen throws a moiré pattern on her face that makes her look unreal and two-dimensional. Like she is being projected onto the windowpane. She doesn't say anything; she knows she won't be allowed. She just stands and stares.

SATURDAY, FEBRUARY 19

Local news outlets have stopped taking my calls and The Times and The Post won't give me the time of day. They all think I'm crazy. I told them I have proof, not just the tapes now, and the police records, but the dead body of Ana 2 in my basement, and Polaroids of Ana 3 standing in my yard. Instead of listening to me, those fools forwarded my information to the police. An officer paid me a visit this morning. He did not have a warrant, and I must have seemed sane enough because he was content to browbeat me on my porch. I promised I would stop making prank calls, while Ana 3 watched us talking from the woods across the street.

Each generation of her is a little less human. As if whatever twisted demiurge is responsible for her regeneration no longer has access to the original model and is working from a memory corrupted by self-projection. This observation has spawned an idea and a plan of action—one revolting in its particulars but certain in its effect. I will pile up a mountain of evidence so high that it can't be ignored. I may get buried beneath, but as the old saying goes, extremis malis extrema remedia.

***

Burke was a colleague of mine, and a childhood friend. We grew up together in Westham and we were both students in the second-ever class at VCU, the year after Richmond Professional Institute merged with the Medical College of Virginia. We graduated and moved out west together in 1973 and cut our teeth 'gofering' dailies to and from the film lab for Hollywood auteurs. Burke got hooked on blow and fell way behind with his dealer, and I helped him get out of it by selling an outtake from *Apocalypse Now* that depicted Marlon Brando teaching a fifteen-year-old Lawrence Fishburne how to castrate a bull calf. I suppose it was my fault for teaching him how much money could be made selling certain kinds of footage, but Burke had always been his own worst enemy. He traded his cocaine habit for an addiction to unearthing footage better left buried, but I wanted a straight career. We parted ways nearly two decades ago, after he moved back to Richmond (read: was chased out of L.A.) and I took a job at the Academy Film Archive. We touched base from time to time, and Burke kept me abreast of all the political bombshells he had helped throw, or in some cases took payment to defuse. The last I heard he was selling framed photos of the Briley brothers' executions to the family members of their ten victims. I figured he had long since given up his quest for the mythical Ana Log, as the tapes became known after an anonymous Richmond cop told the story to a reporter from the Washington Post. The cop apparently changed his mind and the story never ran, but it was later posted to the alt.film.lost Usenet group in early 1990. The author of the piece was not named, but the post alleged that he had later hanged himself. Once he heard about the Ana Log, Burke's personal connection to both Richmond and VCU made him particularly obsessed with finding it. In fact, he returned to Richmond for that express purpose—but he was stonewalled for years by the Richmond P.D., until they finally admitted the case files had gone missing.

I had decided long ago to keep my distance from Burke, which is why I ignored his messages on my machine, even the ones claiming that he had acquired the tapes. I recognized the zeal and then the panic in his voice, but Burke had always been excitable, and I doubted it was as serious or as important as he suggested. Obviously I misjudged.

A few weeks later I was at a conference in D.C., and my conscience was gnawing at me, so instead of flying back to L.A. after it was over I decided to check in on my old friend. I rented a car and drove down on a Friday afternoon; the traffic was so bad it took me nearly four hours, so I was in a terrible mood when I arrived at his place on Old Gun. Burke's ill-gotten gains had bought him an acre of riverfront property on the southside, where he could conduct his transactions in private luxury.

My knocks went unanswered. A little voice in my head told me to try the front door anyway. I don't know where that voice came from, but I wish it had kept quiet. In Burke's den, I found a letter taped to a gargantuan television. It was addressed *"To Whom the Duty Falls"* and contained instructions not to go into the basement until viewing all eight of the tapes and reading the case files and diary he had left on a nearby shelf.

I was exhausted from the drive, but five minutes into Tape #1 I knew it was going to be a long night. When I'd finished, I went down to the basement. Burke always said he was going to find the Ana Log, even if it killed him, so I wasn't exactly surprised to find him dead from his own hand. What did surprise me was the stinking pile of seven progressively more deformed iterations of Ana's corpse that I found down there with him.

When I came back upstairs, I saw a new one standing in Burke's backyard, staring up at the house. She flickers and fades, as if fighting for purchase, and her thick, black edges bleed and smear outward in a baleful aura. Her head is no longer the captain of her body, but an extraneous looking appendage that juts out at an obscene angle. The face on this head is slack and utterly lifeless.

I won't be able to look at her for very long.

WRITTEN ROCK,
WHERE DEIDRE DREED HER WEIRD

The first clear omen was a thin blade of clouds edged in crimson. Deidre only noticed it when she tired of the silence in the car and cracked the passenger window a few kilometers shy of Polatlı. As the air rushed in and chilled her face, the sky pointed westward with a scalpel.

An hour or so from Yazılıkaya, a mother eagle returning to its nest atop a telephone pole marked their passing into the fabled Phrygian Highlands. Deidre could not make out what the eagle had killed or see the fledglings it was feeding, but the stringy strips of flesh hanging from its beak led her down into a dark little place in her mind where she imagined what it felt like both to tear and to be torn apart. While she lingered with those thoughts, all sorts of hoodoos, crags, and natural stone citadels that Turks call *kales* carved the land around them into a gothic mirror of her mood. Villages became more widely spaced and then dwindled away almost entirely. In one outpost a woman stood in her slanted doorway and watched them pass through with the same stony regard one might give to a plastic bag caught in the wind. Even the droll navigator who voiced their GPS, all-seeing eye of every alleyway in Ankara, was struck dumb by this stark erasure of the modern world, offering only a fallback "unnamed road" for every winding stretch of gravel and earth that took them further from the highway. All those miles of desolation numbed them into a daze. With their eyes everywhere else, they missed the first sign that said to park at the edge of the village and approach the site on foot. A second, handmade sign directed them to a dirt lot behind a rustic little cafe. Otherwise empty, save a bored mare tied to a split rail fence. While Tim parked the car to his satisfaction, Deidre fixated on the horse, standing alone in the shadow of an ancient shrine, and wondered what would happen if she released it.

The old woman was shimmying her way over to them before they'd even finished stepping from the car. She wore billowy black pants and a poppy-patterned blouse under a black sweater vest. A plain black headscarf—more *babushka* than *hijab*—framed her stolid face. She carried a glass bottle of Coke in one hand and a plastic bottle of water in the other, along with a grim resolve to sell them both.

"You might want that later," Deidre warned Tim across the roof of the car as he stretched and zipped off his company fleece. When he saw the woman, he turned and tried to deflect her advance with the same warding gesture he used to shoo away the Syrian refugees who camped outside their building.

"Not today," he said. "Maybe next time."

"*Merhaba*," Deidre tried. The woman rewarded her effort with a small cryptic smile before Deidre ducked into the back seat to wake Molly. When she straightened up with the limp bundle in her arms, the woman came forward as if drawn to a holy relic. She spoke with musical bursts and nodded at the end of each refrain. Deidre unconsciously mimicked her nods with feigned comprehension, and yet still felt as if she somehow understood to what she had agreed.

"Should we?" Tim asked, impatient. "Do you need any help?"

"We're fine," Deidre said. She propped Molly on the trunk's edge and offered the old woman a chance to babysit while she retrieved the backpack carrier bearing everything they might conceivably need.

Molly accepted the stranger's hands with the same eerie composure she'd displayed throughout their entire expat experience. She made no sound and her eyes never seemed to blink, ever observing the world through errant strands of hair. Almost everyone who'd met her in infancy commented on how quiet and calm she was, but Deidre wasn't so certain. What others perceived as preternatural serenity presented to her more like watchful caution. Which led to worry over whether her muted child sourced her vigilance from past-life tragedy, or some inchoate idea of what lay ahead for her in this one. The latter notion had of late become a problematic fixation. Four months in and Deidre was still failing to make any sense of their moving again, let alone to a country that neither of them knew much about. Why had Tim's firm insisted on such a sudden re-assignment? Did he do something bad? Was she being punished for it too? Tim didn't like to talk about these things, and only got angry when pressed.

Had they been sent to Istanbul or Izmir, she might have faced the upheaval with a different attitude—hopeful, or at least more ambivalent. But in her personal opinion, Ankara was a frightening and vaguely hostile place. Perched way out on Anatolia's central plateau, its Brutalist architecture and volatile weather patterns gave it an almost monolithic sense of oppression and doom. Like a not-quite-dormant volcano. Or a bank of storm clouds that lingered too long on the horizon, biding time and building power for maximum impact. *What is coming?* she'd asked Molly aloud just the night before. *What does it want with us?* To lure the child towards sleep she dangled her favorite bauble, an amber pendant with a prehistoric ant trapped inside. *Will we know it when it sees us?*

"Are you talking to me?" Tim had asked from the other room. Deidre echoed his question in a stage whisper, and fretted over Molly's refusal to speak.

"Can't we leave that behind this time?" Tim said, still stretching, as if in preparation to run. "How long are we going to be here anyway?" He torqued each elbow with the back of his opposite hand and swiveled his torso.

The empty carrier embarrassed him somehow, even though Deidre was the one always carrying it. She only wore it for backup—for when her arms inevitably tired—but sometimes it seemed as if Molly embarrassed him too. As if his daughter's delayed speech and her slight, underdeveloped body impugned his bloodline somehow. While Deidre finished her preparations, the old woman babbled on like an old friend. As she spoke, one of her gnarled hands flexed open and closed as if squeezing an invisible ball. Deidre donned the backpack and retrieved her threadbare daughter.

"*Geçmiş olsun,*" the woman said in parting. This confused Deidre, as she understood it to be a phrase of sympathy, said to someone ill or about to suffer.

***

Cracked and weathered rafter tails jutted through mudbrick walls along a rough gravel lane. Sounds drifted over the walls—goats and cows and chickens, a faint and intermittent hammering—but they had yet to spy any other inhabitants, save the mare and the old woman. The main attraction leaned over them now, demanding attention if not worship, but Deidre resisted the urge to look until her view was perfect. Instead she focused on the quaint anachronism of the village.

The guidebooks identified the local populace as an enclave of Circassians descending from those forced from the Caucasus during the Tsarist expansion. Many crossed or skirted the Black Sea and resettled along its opposite shore, but some spread further south. Geographic exile, non-Turkic ethnicity, and privately unorthodox beliefs kept them from ever fully assimilating. When they arrived here, the ruins were abandoned and forgotten. A place no one wanted was one where they might at last be safe. Phrygian tombs and Roman niches became their pantries and bedrooms until foreign archaeologists came along to chastise and reclaim. The forced retreat did not back them off far. Their fieldstone walls and stick-woven animal pens still clung to the foothills like dioramas of the ancient habitations they overlaid. Access to the site was granted through the courtyard and open doorway of the docent's house. They found this handsome fellow in an embroidered vest behind a counter of gleaming poplar. Hand-hewn beams lined the ceiling. Lacquered knots and burls peeked up at them from beneath a patchwork of antique kilim rugs. Deidre smelled wool and apple tea. Pamphlets, postcards, and *nazar* amulets stocked a spinning wire display.

"*Hoş geldiniz,*" the man said. "Welcome."

"*Hoş bulduk.*" Deidre's in-kind reply earned her a smirk nearly as wide as his Dalí mustache. There is no literal translation, least none that makes sense out of context, so she turned the implied meaning around and around in her head to be sure she'd used it correctly. *It pleases me to be here.*

The man held up both hands, callused and splayed. Tim furnished the lira without complaint, for a change. Then the man either mistook Deidre's pleasantry for greater proficiency or else lacked the English to choose otherwise. He spoke for some time, and appeared to be advising them on what to look for on their tour, but none of his words meant anything to her. His pantomime helped, however, and he finished with an index finger tracing a circle on his other palm. Deidre's imperfect understanding turned on a caution to take the path clockwise, lest they run afoul of some guard or custodian who might otherwise take offense. His duties complete, the man gestured at a ledger. Tim behaved all along as if he were being sold something, and drifted away with that same dismissive wave—but Deidre knew from her reading that these far-flung sites depended on visitor statistics for their government funding. She signed for three, using imaginary names that came to mind only seconds after the idea itself. If asked why she did this, she would have sworn she didn't know.

Back outside, the primary monument was on a cliff face not far from the docent's house. A few minutes of uninformed staring were enough for Tim, but Deidre held Molly and lingered a long while beneath it. Molly's cottony skin smelled faintly of Cheerios and bubble gum shampoo. Her hair was wild and wind-tangled, but

Deidre let it be rather than break their embrace. They rocked slightly beneath the monument, as if swaying to a song only they could hear.

Nameless masters had carved a giant temple façade upon the terminating spur of the plateau. The pillars and pediment were in slightly higher relief, incised with diamonds and squiggles. Housed inside this frame was an unsolvable maze of interlocking patterns. Dimly understood Paleo-Phrygian inscriptions ran across the top and down the right in a jagged script. If nothing else, Deidre's library science degree left her with a robust definition of research. She'd been studying the site in general, and this relief in particular, for several weeks. Most of the available sources in English were either dated or muddied by academic jargon. In the flesh, off the cuff, she decided it was meant to function like a massive mental gate, and the space inside some kind of conceptual labyrinth, intelligible only to the initiated. Deidre glanced up to the place where the apex of the temple curled into crescents, or goat horns. The 'acroterion', she thought it was called. Erosion or earthquake or some other violence had wormed a crack between the horns and begun to split the monument apart. Short lengths of bolted iron spliced the fissure, but the repair looked haphazard and insufficient. Thanks to her insistence on an early start, they had arrived while the late-morning sun still hit the monument dead on. The effect was striking enough to make the glow appear to be coming from inside the rock itself. As if this giant slab of volcanic tuff was flashing back to the purer reds and oranges of its igneous youth, back before it had cooled to a dimmer default shade. When the light show was over, Deidre took Molly over to the false door inset where the monument touched the earth and lifted her child into the niche. Earlier pilgrims had assumed it was an actual door to an actual tomb. A cognate of *Midas* in the most prominent inscription suggested a famous occupant and cemented a misleading association with the legendary king. Centuries of vandalism and looting sprung from this one intractable idea. King Midas may have funded the monument, but Deidre knew its real patron was the figure now missing from this niche. Apt in her absence, always consigned to ruins and steeped in historical shadow. An eroding graffito in the niche named this legitimate contender for the most ancient deity of them all. Statuary found at truly ancient sites like Çatalhöyük attested her worship to at least 8000 BC. Known by other names in other places but here, in her homeland, she was the *Matar Kubileya*. Mother of the Mountain.

"It's dangerous over here," Tim shouted as Deidre drifted over with Molly. "Don't come this way."

In a rare gesture of good faith that Deidre guessed was on a list somewhere of tips for international businessmen, Tim granted his wife say over their first vacation in country. Even so, he couldn't help but try to shepherd the discussion. While she waffled, he suggested Istanbul, or Cappadocia, or a rented villa somewhere along the Turquoise Coast. He'd heard great things about Kaş and Antalya. Instead she chose a site and a region that very few people on Earth could place on a map, let alone find reason to visit.

He'd been climbing around a pockmarked outcrop to their right, and his voice faded into echo as he ducked into another chamber. The feature was half dwelling, half mausoleum, if Dierdre remembered correctly. Dizzyingly intricate and innately disturbing. Not because the living kept their dead so close, but because it reminded her of something horrible—some mazing prison she'd survived by going deep within herself and pretending she wasn't there. She tried and tried to fish it to the surface, but all that came to mind in the moment was that big Swiss cheese play structure where she sometimes hid during grade school recess when the other kids were being jerks. Smelled like it too. Pee and loneliness. As she wandered closer, odor and memory worked their dark magic until the smell of urine grew so overwhelming she feared she might vomit. Only when she heard him zip up did she realize Tim was the one waving the wand. The goddamn WC was marked and still visible outside the docent's house. Deidre grumbled and carried Molly another direction in disgust.

Iron grates covered the biggest of the holes underfoot, but still left a minefield of pit traps and drop-offs. With the nearest hospital several hours away, Deidre agreed and took Molly back the way they'd come. A small plaque nearly at ground level identified the outcrop as *Kırkgöz*, or *The Cave of Forty Eyes*. Like that wasn't capital C creepy. Deidre panned a 360, and the empty grandeur of the place settled a little deeper into her bones. Phantom assemblages of rock and shadow stared back at her en masse.

"This place is weird," Tim said from somewhere above them.

Hysteria bubbled up through Deidre's esophagus and threatened to escape into a cackle. Her wee Scottish grandmother and beloved namesake had once taught her an older, deeper meaning of the word, and Tim's incidental utterance was so apt it was almost an invocation.

Weird began its slow semantic drift as a synonym for fate. Immutable and inexorable. Back then it was often paired with an even hoarier verb, to *dree*, which in Scottish meant to submit or endure, but in Indo European was closer to an act of service to one's tribe. This one very old and haunted phrase—*to dree one's weird*—worked an essential magic for Deidre. It gave her windblown life not just a shape and a path, but the whiff of classical pathos.

While Dierdre projected, Tim finished his desecration. He emerged from the back and looked over towards Deidre but something about her posture or bearing—the way she clung to Molly with such ferocious desperation—must have bothered him, because soon he was not only heading up the path away from them but walking in the wrong direction.

"Wait!" Deidre said, but he was already out of earshot unless she shouted. And to shout in this place seemed in some ways even worse than pissing on it. Molly seemed to sense her alarm. She soothed the child and said in a cheery voice, "Let's play a game, shall we? We can go the other way and meet Daddy in the middle."

And so that's what they did.

Only the lefthand path was more meandering and less easy to follow. It led them down so many curious offshoots that reuniting with Tim was soon replaced by more immediate urges. A Roman-era necropolis cratered the entire eastern flank of the plateau. Dozens of graceful arcosolia curved over individual cist tombs, some in the cliff face and some in full-blown chamber tombs leading deep into the rock. Inscriptions, benches, sacrificial altars, and other strange stone workings awaited their inspection. So many features it became impossible to differentiate the natural from the fashioned. Every irregularity invited exploration and creative ideation.

Another southerly path ushered them under the lee of *kale* and left them deliciously lost in shadow. There, in a gloomy little glade, they found and traced a large inscription facing away from the path, as if to hide it. They found another false doorway that someone had dubbed The Hyacinth Monument. In Turkish the flower's name was *Sümbüllü* and to Deidre it sounded like mumbled rumors of a more exotic Narnia; one with far stranger definitions of Turkish delight. The decorative patterns were so pretty and distinctive that Deidre lifted Molly into the threshold and took a picture of her leaning stiffly inside, head propped on the patterned rock and thin pale arms against her sides. But when viewed on her phone it looked like her precious girl was lying in a sarcophagus—an impression only strengthened by the large stone balanced overhead, threatening to seal her inside. The idea disturbed her so much she deleted the photo.

While they went in search of something called The Broken Monument, they missed Tim's hurried descent from the *kale* along a natural ramp. A few seconds later Deidre heard him calling her name, but she'd decided by then to make him pay for his earlier disregard. Soon his strident calls were fading again, and with them any feeling of remorse. Once he was gone, she and Molly doubled back and climbed the same stone slope. It carried them gradually upward along a ritual way adorned with small figural reliefs, many-legged things, and odd little people with perfectly round heads and cylindrical bodies, like playing pieces in a board game. On top of the *kale*, time slipped its tether entirely and they had the most wondrous afternoon. The granite plateau offered a commanding view for miles. Tall grasses growing from the thin soil swayed in the steady breeze like the gathered host at a revival. The low murmur of their rustling filled the austere landscape with something more like a presence than an absence—a collective and contagious reverence for all the centuries of ritual conducted here. They found rain puddles in shallow basins that bloomed with algae supernovas. A step throne with seating for two and more boardgame people carved into the seatbacks. Only these seemed more clearly female, as their bowl-cut hair tipped up into the cutest little curls. How great and how right was a throne for girls? How strange and how curious that it boasted two heads but only one body! Deidre and Molly leaned against these figured seatbacks, closed their eyes, and let the sun warm their thoughts and faces.

Eons of wind on the soft rock had sculpted several prominent formations into seals and camels and humpbacked whales. The menagerie lured them so far from the tourist path that they disappeared again from view. During Tim's manic second pass, they snacked on raisins and pizza-flavored goldfish crackers with their backs against the whale's warm back. Molly seemed content to sit and doze while Deidre gazed into the distance and barely resisted a craving to wander that wilderness. Three more *kales* at staggered remove cut up the horizon like watchtowers on a signal path. She could not remember the last time she felt so charmed by a place. So correct in a choice. All afternoon she'd felt far less eager to find her husband than worried of when they would. On a wide flat scarp that quirked their sense of scale, Deidre's arms grew too tired to carry the child any further, and her decision to bring the carrier was justified, as usual. She threaded Molly's little legs through the seat holes and used a stone ledge to more easily put it on again. They walked onward as one body with two heads.

On the backside of the plateau they found one of the site's rare nods to modern improvement. Skilled carpenters had eased a tricky way down with a cascading network of wooden stairs and landings. Only it seemed they forgot a railing. Even so, it wasn't worry over falling with Molly on her back that halted Deidre, or the realization that they'd nearly completed the loop and still not rendezvoused with Tim. It was a palpable spike in the sense of being watched.

She looked down and saw that klatches of two or three near duplicates of the woman from the parking lot now stood on nearly every ledge and niche about the site below them. Still more shuffled into position before assuming that same affectless pose. From this distance their scarves obscured their faces and rendered their heads as ovals. Atop their shadowy bodies they looked very much like the schematic figures Deidre had seen inscribed into the stone.

Already quiet, the world now went utterly silent. Molly reacted by lurching in the carrier as if trying to leap from her back. The force of it toppled them both forward. Deidre teetered on the landing and fought to regain her balance. Every step down felt too fast and out of control. Again and again her balance was thrown by Molly's eagerness to eject herself out of the carrier. The gathering stayed motionless throughout Deidre and Molly's lurching descent. They stood so quiet and still that Deidre began to wonder if they were just figments of her anxiety. Perhaps they would fade if she only gave them closer attention—but she dared not look away from her feet long enough to be certain.

She only lifted her eyes again when she was back on more stable ground. In closer proximity the gathering stayed solid and real, but lost its monolithic aspect. She found she could more easily differentiate them. Tall and short. Round and thin. Old and if not exactly young, then not nearly as old as that. Nothing scary or inimical, just stoic faces and sad eyes. The elation she'd felt on the *kale* left her like a stolen breath. Now she felt tired and sad and cold. Molly kicked and squirmed within the carrier, still begging to be put down.

Deidre walked on, for what else could she do? The women gave no sign to make their wishes known. Past more tombs and arcosolia. Past strange small holes cut high into the rock with no discernible purpose. Past the site's most monumental tomb, now sealed off with metal bars, where beautiful stone beds ran foot to head beneath a gabled roof like an invitation to an eternal slumber party.

Eventually she reached the last astounding feature that she had not yet seen. Carved deep into the stone, a twisting umbilical cord of a staircase led upwards to a votive cave and downwards to a ritual pit. Another gauntlet of village women led to it and lined its upper half, giving her no choice but to follow the only route they left for her.

The steps were steep and nearly worn away. Deidre just managed not to stumble despite the child thrashing on her back. On a small ledge at the top, she crouched and finally freed the imp. Deidre cautioned her to stay close while setting her down. When the child slipped over towards the lip of the votive cave, Deidre grabbed her limp arms again with ramping fear and frustration. Molly twisted away and her head lolled until her neck nearly folded in two. As if she were boneless and the person who touched her more monster than mother. The bite was quick and painful; it surprised Deidre and made her let go. When the child dropped away and slid into the cave, Deidre was still too shocked to follow.

***

When the blackness cleared Deidre realized she was still on the steps, kneeling down and screaming Molly's name into the cave. Her diaphragm kinked and cramped in pain. Everything above her neck was dipped into darkness. From above she would have looked decapitated. One body with no head.

It took her some time to realize Tim was crouched there beside her, gripping her arm so forcefully his fingernails cut bloody half-moon dents through her jacket. Her face stung and she didn't know why until Tim yanked her upright and slapped her again. Hard enough to leave his hand on her face.

"Stop it! You're making a scene! Where the hell have you been?"

Nothing drove him crazier than public embarrassment. He started shaking her so hard she felt the water slosh in her stomach. She didn't fight back. Fighting back only made it worse. Better to follow Molly's lead and suffer it all in silence…

Oh dear God, Molly.

Deidre stopped screaming and swiveled her head. The village women had vanished. The carrier was empty save a homemade doll done up in Molly's likeness.

"Where's Molly?" she said in a dead voice, and that's what finally stopped him. Instead of looking around for his daughter Tim just stared into Deidre's eyes, as if to find her there. Deidre hated the way his eyes made her feel, and she broke the gaze to look over his shoulder, into the mouth of the mountain. "Where is Molly?" she said again.

"Don't do this to me. You know where she is."

"What does that mean?"

The waning day reached into the darkness of the cavity, just enough light to trace some small dim shape or effigy. Crouching or misshapen. Familiar but hostile.

"I give up," Tim said. "This isn't worth it anymore."

With no forethought or design beyond freeing herself and recovering Molly, Deidre lifted both arms with such speed and ferocity it broke Tim's grip and knocked him back a step. At this sudden prompt, something shifted in the configuration of the cave. Layers of shadow collapsed and the depth of blackness flattened. What was a cave was now niche, empty and at most a meter deep. The mountain swallowed the rest.

Disgorged from its throat, something coiled and fluttering shot from the niche and flew at Tim. Birds or bats or bees. Disturbed and self-defensive. Already teetering, eyes bugging, Tim flailed, failed to recover, and fell over backwards like a man pushed into a well.

There was a moment when Deidre probably could have stayed his fall, but her eyes never left the niche, not even as Tim ragdolled the entire length of the stone staircase. A lot less sound than expected attended the plummet. He never even screamed.

Before he gurgled back to consciousness; before he called her something horrid; before he faked another apology and begged her to summon a rescue that would never come; before he whimpered about how cold it was down there, how scary the death-shaped thing looming over him; before she gave in to mercy or fell down there herself, Deidre turned and hugged the mountain. Facing away, she never saw what took him. The coldest, darkest part of her wished he would live long enough to experience some measure of the pain he had caused, but mostly she hoped the Mother would accept her offering and reveal a way forward. Whatever that might be.

***

The café owner knew a good trade when offered one. A new foreign car for a tired old horse was a fair deal no matter what was hidden in the small print. They consummated the exchange over a cold glass of *rakı* and a warm piece of the house *börek*.

Deidre did not mount the mare, merely laid her empty backpack carrier across its more ample shoulders and led it gingerly from the village. A small contingent of the women escorted her into the next valley, but no one spoke, not even when they bade her goodbye.

The mare's comforting flank cut the rising wind and radiated enough warmth to put some distance behind Deidre before she needed to make camp and light a fire with the kindling they had provided her. Walking into the wilderness at night with something larger and more powerful than herself excited her in ways she no longer needed to articulate. Not with old Scottish words, or even older ones in Phrygian.

The Rememberist

When I was a boy, my mother warned me away from my wicked interests lest they overcome my better nature. But alas, I did not heed her. As a man I have learned to keep them on a short tether, and only let out the slack when the occasion warrants. Verily has my vocation been a blessing for that. Forty-two years of calamity reportage have allowed me to feed and shelter my unhealthy fixations behind the caul of journalism, but they have also taught me that the unwashed masses share a large measure of my predilection—enough at least to double sales of the *Dispatch* whenever one of my grislier columns darkens the page. And though shortages of certain items became commonplace in Richmond as Union forces marched closer, we never lacked in news of the terrible. Of that we had a-plenty, particularly in the summer of '63, when I finally slaked my thirst for the unspeakable and discovered that there are things which even I cannot abide.

I was living on Fourth Street at the time, in a small flat above an unscrupulous apothecary. This afforded me ample opportunity both to witness and be victimized by all manner of common crime. With no less than three brothels, five pubs, and two gambling houses within a short stroll, easy marks with carefree pockets were plentiful around Shockoe after sunfall. Misdemeanors, however, did not interest me much. I sought the mark of Cain, as I was known to exclaim too often and too loudly to anyone within earshot after a pint too many of Alsopp's Most Excellent Ale. And by that I meant gruesome turns of fate and violent acts of passion. Like the octoroon house girl who poisoned fourteen Shiffletts over in Cumberland, only to fall victim to a water moccasin while making her escape. Or when Second Lieutenant Scott of the Virginia Cavalry entertained his men one night during the Battle of Chancellorsville by donning the garb of a dead Yankee and dancing through camp, only to have his Negro boy run him through with his own sword.

Duels were also excellent fodder, with their requisite backstories and often mortal conclusions, but *affaires d'honneur* were seldom occasioned after the start of the war, and they ceased entirely once Dragonierre opened his fencing gallery over on 10th and Main and invited gentlemen to settle their scores in a less deadly fashion *AT ANY TIME, DAY OR NIGHT!* Courage seemed to be leaking out of our nobles like black bile from a punctured spleen. By March, the number of petitions for substitutes outnumbered those beseeching aid in tracking down escaped slaves. I do not blame them, I suppose (nor for that matter the runaways); if I were wealthy I might have done the same, had my brother's errant axe fall not rendered me *de facto* unfit, but I do question the wisdom of advertising one's cowardice to the general public. If the Confederacy had not outlawed the practice later that year, the war might have ended much sooner for lack of men to fight it.

The explosion at the munitions laboratory on Brown's Island was still raw in the public mind at the time, though the wounds of the survivors had healed as much as Mother Nature could manage. It is hard to imagine a worse blow to our city's morale than thirty dead daughters and nearly two score more left burned and scarred beyond recognition. Several days after the accident I tried to locate Mary Ryan, the young Irish girl who precipitated the tragedy by banging too hard on a canon primer, but her parents refused to let me see her. Poor Mary died a few days later. I did succeed in interviewing Cornelia Mitchell at General Hospital No. 2, and shall never forget the hellish light that blazed in her one unscalded eye as it seared me through her veil of gauze. The incessant moaning of the other victims testified to the unbearable pain they were all enduring, but Ms. Mitchell seemed intent to suffer in silence. I asked her to describe the moments after the explosion, and she focused her eye on a point somewhere over my head and said she *would rather not, thank you.* With a little more cajoling and sympathetic murmuring I learned that she was not among the dozen or so who ran towards the river, but instead broke off—pell-mell and still ablaze—in the direction of the main munitions depot, and almost certainly would have annihilated everyone not already killed in the initial detonation had a clearer thinking foreman not tackled and extinguished her in time. It is exactly this sort of detail that I seek when I settle on a topic—the kind that lingers in the mind long after the general particulars fade. Should I fail to find one in fact, I am not above growing my own in fiction's fertile soil. So long as the result does not slander any otherwise upstanding citizen or steal away a story's essential truth, then I feel no shame in doing so. That being said, the following account neither requires nor would brook even the smallest degree of elaboration. It is, I swear, the God's honest truth.

One of my duties at the *Dispatch* was to generate the Amusements column, which catalogued the various and sundry entertainments available, and occasionally to write reviews of the same. Those of lesser means or greater dignity might be surprised to learn that large numbers of ladies and gentlemen continued throughout the war to regularly attend frivolities like Buckley and Company's Southern Nightingale Opera & Farce Troupe, or the juvenile antics of Rascal Tim. The New Richmond Theater had just opened in February that year, and by all accounts its seats were nearly full for every performance. Perhaps the distractions helped ease anxieties about marauding Yanks. How else to explain the popularity of mechanized falderal like Lee Mallory's

Pantechnoptomon, which commanded standing room attendance at Metropolitan Hall, and which proudly and boldly depicted:

JACKSON CROSSING THE POTOMAC!
Also, the Scenic-Automatic Spectacle of
CAMP AND FIELD LIFE IN VIRGINIA,
And that wonder of mechanical skill,
THE WOUNDED OFFICER and his FAITHFUL HORSE!

With ample doses of real-life bloodshed delivered daily to their very doorsteps, it is more than curious that our supposed betters found the stomach to seek out more, however abstracted and defanged by melodramatic accoutrement. Additional proof, I suppose, that we are all morbid creatures at heart. And yet I must admit that there is something undeniable about the way a simulacrum can seize the mind and play wondrous tricks on one's sense of reality. In my youth I had often heard tell of the time when Johann Mälzel brought the Turk, his famous automaton chess master, to our fair city and vexed all who witnessed it, including no less a mind than that of our unfortunate Mr Poe. Early in my career I was able to witness in Philadelphia the exhibition of Joseph Faber's Euphonia, and have been haunted ever since by the memory of that otherworldly voice emanating from a disembodied head. Yet even those masterful contrivances pale in comparison to the miraculous nightmare of Philus Eisen.

I'll never know to whom I owe my introduction. A scrap of paper was left on my desk one day bearing, in nearly illegible scrawl, a simple advisory: *You will not want to miss the show tonight at The Very Bottom.* I am not ashamed to admit I knew the place. As a single man, with normal needs, I did occasionally dip my pen into some of Shockoe's public women, but more often satisfied myself with a bawdy performance, which is exactly what under normal circumstances would have been offered that night at this particular establishment. And so it was that with severely misguided expectations, I sauntered down to the corner of Twelfth and Arch where The Very Bottom squatted unsteadily over the canal on its mossy brick haunches like a lady making water. Something about the scene immediately struck me as more perverted than usual. I had acquired a tincture of McMunn's Opium Elixir from my apothecary neighbor, as I found a few drops helped me enjoy the shows without the lingering discomfort of unspent lust, so initially I blamed the distorting effects of the narcotic—but the more I looked, the more I noticed that none of the normal gaiety attended the men (for it was all men and no couples, temporary or otherwise) who instead stood morosely in line awaiting entry, heads down or hidden behind hats pulled tight. A small placard had been posted by the entrance that read in sum:

Philus Eisen,
The Rememberist

I found my place in the queue and wondered aloud who had died, which earned me several gloomy stares from my peers. It was only then that I detected the source of my disquiet in the odd demographics of the men around me. Fully one in four lacked a limb. Most wanted an arm and had sleeves pinned to coats which cleverly hid their deficiency, but I also noted at least two men on crutches with missing legs. The sight of men diminished by their service was no rarity by then, but never so many in one place. As if harkened, a phantom pain rejoined from the two missing fingers on my right hand, and I crammed the hand even deeper than usual into my pocket to quiet it. Then the doors opened, we paid our fare, and we were let inside.

Absent were the two-bit pianist and the jaunty prelude that normally greeted me as I entered the dingy old theater. In their place was a tense and somber silence. Instead of lantern footlights, tall candlesticks lined the stage with a flickering glow. The sparse crowd took their seats, and in short order the show began.

An old man in a surgeon's smock wheeled a gurney onstage, which supported a younger gentleman with dark curly hair. A tarp had been laid down and the old man positioned the gurney on top. From a shelf on the bottom he retrieved a black leather satchel and laid it on the gurney. From inside the satchel he withdrew a clamping tourniquet apparatus, a long thin knife, and a bone saw with an ivory grip. He then wrapped the tourniquet around the upper-right arm of the man on the gurney, inserted the end through the buckle, pulled it taut, and tightened the clamp with multiple twists. His preparations apparently complete, the old man stepped aside and the man on the gurney addressed the audience.

"What you are about to see is a recreation of a field hospital amputation from March of last year, during the first engagement at Kernstown. Private William Attison of the 5th Virginia Cavalry lost most of his right bicep muscle to a Minié ball. It was decided that the arm must be removed to save Private Attison's life. One of three such operations that day."

Without further ado, the old man ambled back to the gurney, picked up the knife and made several quick incisions. As he leaned over the patient, it was impossible to see exactly what was happening—but blood was soon trickling down the gurney and pooling on the tarp. My breath caught short in my throat, and I swiveled my head to gauge the reaction of my peers and help determine exactly what I witnessing, but the few around me looked on with stone faces. The old man then stepped back and allowed us to see what he had done.

A flap of the younger's man skin had been cut and peeled back to reveal the raw pink muscle beneath. The old man turned back to his charge and again made quick work with his knife. Another pause and some dabbing with gauze to show us the severed muscle and the white of the bone, and again the man on the gurney addressed the audience, his breathing a bit labored but otherwise under control.

"We require two volunteers from the audience."

I leaked an involuntary laugh at the absurd request, but arms shot up all around me. All of a sudden, I remembered that I was attending a performance. The thorned vine of revulsion that had been growing up my spine blossomed into rapt fascination. I raised my arm, sheepishly at first, but then with all the avidity of tack-sharp schoolchild. Had I not been chosen that night, I might have limited to that one memorable encounter my exposure to the cursed Mr Eisen, but life has a curious way of giving us what we think we need. The old man pointed to me and another man, and up to the stage I went. I expected to be less convinced of the conceit the closer I approached, but the opposite proved true. In short order I was staring down into the man's carven sinew like a mesmerist's marionette.

"Hold my shoulders firmly please. And do not let go."

The younger man's voice snapped me back to task, and I placed my hands on his shoulders as directed.

"Harder," he growled.

I looked down to see that he was staring me straight in the face with a delirious intensity, his jaw muscles pulsing behind clenched teeth, lips pulled back like a cornered tomcat. I bore down on his shoulders with all my weight, pinning him to the gurney. My cohort did the same with his wrist.

Then the old man began to saw.

Between the sound of the steel abrading the bone and the bucking convulsions of the victim beneath me, I very nearly lost control of my senses. But the whole operation was over in a minute. My fellow assistant had been holding so firmly onto the arm in question that he fell over backwards when it was riven, and he landed on his rear end with the severed appendage in his lap. He shivered it up and away from him as if it might strike, and then he scrambled away in mortal fear. The old attendant calmly picked up the arm and displayed it to the audience like a rabbit he had produced from a hat. Then he placed it on the shelf beneath the gurney and began to apply a bandage to the wound.

"You can let up now," said the man beneath me.

I looked at him, and for a second I was afraid to set him free. There was a deranged zeal in his eyes and I recoiled as I realized he had not uttered a single cry or moan. His man helped steady him upright through a period of apparent lightheadedness. Blood was leaking thickly from the stump and soaking the bandage despite the tourniquet, and I wondered why the wound had not been sutured. From somewhere beneath his smock the old man produced a plug of tobacco and handed it to his patient, who inserted it in his gum with his remaining hand. Then the one-armed man addressed the audience once more.

"Private Attison survived the surgery, but succumbed to infection and fever eleven days later. Tonight's performance is dedicated to his memory. One week from tonight, we will remember the fate of Corporal Anders of Company H."

With that the man bowed, lay back on the gurney, and his partner wheeled him off the stage.

Absolutely nothing about the proceedings smacked of trickery. If anything, I felt it lacked a modicum of showmanship. Several years earlier, as research for a story on the booming market for cadavers, I had attended an autopsy at the Medical College of Virginia. Excepting the use of a live subject, Eisen's show bore a remarkable resemblance. Immediately I knew that I must speak to him and glean his purpose for mutilating himself. As the others in the crowd filed out, I made my way to the stage door and knocked. When it became clear that no response was forthcoming, I tried the knob and found it unlocked. Down a dim hallway I passed through an empty dressing room and another unlocked door that deposited me back outside, in an alley opposite the theater's entrance, at the foot of some steps. Up these steps, I knew, was a one-room flat. It is unimportant why I knew this, for it has no bearing on the present matter, but suffice it to say that I also knew there was a bed in this apartment, that it creaked something awful, and that it's creaking had a distracting habit of animating the roaches in residence. In any case, I climbed those steps and at the top found yet another door not only unlocked but slightly ajar. Through the crack I saw the aforementioned bed and next to it the dismembered man lying on his back in a pine box filled with dark and loamy earth, with only his head above. For a second I thought him dead, but the patch of dirt on his chest rose and fell with the rhythm of his breathing. Transfixed by this charnel tableau, I stood staring through the crack until a wizened face appeared in the door and nearly stopped my heart.

"I'm… a reporter with *The Dispatch*," I stammered. "I wish to speak with that man."

The old man gave me nothing in return but his inscrutable regard. He stood mute and immobile as a telamon.

"Come back next week," said the man in the box, as if half asleep. "Find me in the bar before the show."

Then the door was closed in my face.

*****

That week lasted longer than certain entire years of my life. It proved impossible to work. I busied myself trying to ascertain who had left me the note, but no one at the paper would admit to it, nor did anyone seem to know the first thing about any unusual performances being staged in the city. Friday rolled around at last, and all day I felt gloomily certain I had seen the last of Eisen—but no, there he was sitting at the bar at The Very Bottom, gripping a glass of whiskey with the very same hand on the very same arm I had seen sawn off with my very own eyes. He looked up at me as I approached, and he reached out with the arm in question wearing a slightly pixilated smile on his face.

"Philus Eisen," he said, shaking my hand.

His grip was limp, and a disagreeable softness in the texture of his palm triggered a quick retraction on my part. I introduced myself, and gave my professional credentials. He invited me to sit with him and have a whiskey, which he acquired with a word to the bartender, who complied but seemed unable or unwilling to look Eisen in the face. I can understand why. It is hard to put into words, but Eisen looked *ruined* somehow. Like a mongrel dog beaten beyond the capacity for loyalty, or a young war widow forced to remarry for support. And yet, amid the forced laughter of the whores and all those God-fearing men getting loudly and unabashedly drunk, the events of the Friday before seemed but a midnight delusion washed away in morning light.

"So it *was* a trick?"

"No."

"Pardon me, an *illusion*."

"No, I say."

"I don't understand."

"Neither do I."

"So you sewed it back on? Your partner must be the greatest surgeon in history."

"Bastian? He butchered my hogs before the war..." Eisen seemed to drift off a moment in reverie, as if he had forgotten I was there. His face softened, and for a very brief time whatever darkness he carried with him seemed to lift. Then, like a shutter dropping, the shade was upon him again and he fixed me with a cruel stare. "I feed them to his dogs, actually. They have quite a taste for it by now."

I sipped my whiskey and digested the implications of *them* and *it*.

"I give up then. Am I supposed to believe that you sprouted a new arm?"

He unbuttoned his shirt sleeves and rolled them back. Then he displayed the bare arms to me in tandem. The left was matted with mature black hairs, and had sinewy contours suggesting muscles and tendons beneath. The right was soft, hairless, and nearly translucent, like the grub of a June bug.

"Fascinating," I stated, for it was, but it was also nauseating.

"Look closer," he invited. I leaned in as he laid the arm atop the bar. I could not be certain, for the light in the place was insufficient, but it seemed as if the arm was growing incrementally more material and less like a thing unearthed from a subterranean lake. I described it as hairless, for I swear it was just moments before, but as I watched a few thin hairs broke through his pores and thickened into life.

I raised my hand and ordered another whiskey. "Make it a double."

I turned back to my companion, who was staring at me with that same queer smile on his face. I mistook him for drunk, but another kind of mischief was at work behind his eyes. I noticed then that his shirt collar was open, and that snaking around his neck was a jagged pink scar. He saw where my eyes had fallen and raised the back of that fetal hand to rub the scar, and seemed ready to speak, but before he could something over my shoulder caught his eye. I followed his gaze to find Bastian standing in a doorway behind the bar, and the utterly emotionless way the old man nodded to Eisen filled me with a terrible foreboding.

"Enjoy the show," Philus laughed and rose from his seat. "It's on me." As he passed me he pressed a chit into my hand. Then he followed Bastian through the door.

***

I am thankful for two reasons that I did not volunteer to aid in the performance that night. For one, it would have ruined my career, if not my reputation. For another, I am not certain I would have left the stage with my mind intact. Those few minutes in the bar with Eisen had left me feeling like a storm was fast approaching and brief flashes of lightning were firing off in the distance, silhouetting the shape of something monstrous on the horizon.

"Tonight we remember Lieutenant Corporal Grayson Anders, a graduate of the Albermarle Military Institute and member of Company H, 13th Tennessee Infantry. While bravely serving at Shiloh, Corporal Anders had the misfortune of having his left foot and lower leg crushed by cannon recoil. There was little choice but to remove the damaged segment."

Eisen again remained silent as his assistant sawed off his left leg just above the knee. The operation took longer this time, and required more force. At one point Bastion had to employ a vicious looking pair of snips to cut through some of tougher sections of the femur. Towards the end, one of the men pinning Eisen fainted dead away. He was left where he fell, for there were more pressing matters at hand. Instead of watching the action, which was quite frankly beginning to sicken me, I chose to focus on the fallen man. He came around in a minute or two, and after he sat up began to rub his brow incessantly as if a blot or stain there, somewhere just behind his forehead, demanded instant removal. Eventually conceding failure, he rose unsteadily to his feet and exited the building without looking back. I wish with all my heart that I had summoned the good sense to do the same.

After the operation was complete, Eisen invited the audience to approach the stage and inspect the severed leg while Bastian packed the wound with rags. Only a few obliged, but they did so with the wide-eyed reverence of pilgrims. It was while these men were recessing back to their seats that a commotion erupted at the back of the theater. I swiveled my head to see a company of police barge in and march down the aisle. Two of them climbed the stage, immediately bent Bastian and the remaining volunteer over the gurney, and put them in handcuffs. Eisen had somehow managed to get down from the gurney, and I saw Captain Weaver grab him as he tried to drag himself to the stage door. Weaver knew me a little and liked me less, and I crouched down in my seat with the hope of hiding my face. The other police began to usher the small crowd from the theater. I joined the exodus and kept my head down, but just before the door I looked back at the stage. Eisen was still struggling mightily to escape and Weaver was beating him down with a billy club. The severed leg still sat at the stage lip, seemingly unnoticed.

***

By all rights that should have ended my gruesome little affair with Eisen, but a few days later I got word at the office that I was wanted by Captain Weaver at Chimborazo. I hailed a coach to the recently completed hospital, way out on the east end of town, just past the city line. It was my first visit, and despite the circumstances I found myself marveling at the massive network of individual wards built on a forty-acre plateau across from Bloody Run Creek. One of Weaver's deputies met me at the gate and escorted me to a building at the back of the hospital, at the far end of a single row of wards running perpendicular to and set off from the main grid. The deputy walked me to the door, and then stood to the side at attention with another guard. Inside I found Eisen in bed looking pale and gazing morosely out the window. A sheet covered him to the waist, but I could tell by its asymmetrical drape that he still lacked a leg. Weaver was facing Eisen, in a chair by the bed. He stood as I entered and took me outside. We nodded at one another but did not shake hands.

"I extended you a courtesy, Harlan, by not sending one of my men for you and embarrassing you at your place of employment, but my well of good graces is only so deep. I need to know the nature of your relationship with this man."

"I have none."

"He says otherwise. In fact, he patently refuses to speak to anyone but you."

"I am not sure what help I can be, Captain. We spoke briefly at a bar last night. He introduced himself as Philus Eisen."

"Impossible."

For a second I thought that Weaver was calling me a liar.

"Eisen died in Castle Thunder over a year ago."

I raised my eyebrows at the mention of the infamous prison, but said nothing.

"Against my better judgment I am prepared to make a deal with you, Harlan. I want you to interview this man and see what you can find out. When I am finished with him, you can use whatever you want in one of your... *columns*." He spat the last word as if it tasted of manure.

I had little choice but to comply, but room enough to protect myself. "He won't talk with you in the room."

Weaver had anticipated me, and was already walking away. "If he tells you anything at all, I expect a full report."

I started towards the door.

"I'm leaving my men here to keep an eye on you both," the Captain threw back at me as he departed.

Eisen was still staring out the window when I came back inside.

"Byrd wasn't far from here when he named Richmond."

I settled into the chair and took out my notebook. "Is that so?"

Eisen nodded, still not looking at me. "There's a spot a little ways up, where the topography mirrors a bend in the Thames near our city's namesake. Funny how we hope to make a thing familiar by just giving it a familiar name."

"And your namesake, this Eisen fellow, what made you want to take the name of a criminal?"

"I took nothing. Criminal or not, he is I and I am him."

"Weaver says Eisen died at Castle Thunder."

"And so he did," Eisen conceded. A weariness had overcome him. "I know what you're after, Harlan, and I am prepared to give it to you, but you must do something for me first."

It was fortunate for me that they had put Eisen by himself in a building set off from the rest, for no one had a vantage to witness me climb through the window with an empty sack from the ward's linen closet and begin filling it with earth. I felt the insanity of what I was doing, whether folly or sorcery, but it was too late to turn back now. I climbed back over the sill and helped Eisen secure the bag around his stump with his belt. Afterwards he leaned back with a sigh, and then he began to speak. His tale was long and meandering, and the deeper into it he got the more he sounded like a madman. I include here the gist of what I eventually communicated to Captain Weaver.

***

When the war broke, Eisen was a general physician serving a small community in Midlothian. His younger brother Johan, of whom he was extremely fond, decided to enlist, and when he died at Bull Run from what Eisen later determined was the shoddy treatment of a relatively minor wound, Eisen realized his services were desperately needed.

"I thought I could save them all," he said simply, palms up.

So he joined up in late '61, and at first he just ministered to those brought back to Richmond, but his skill did not go unnoticed and soon enough he was moved to the front lines. He was present at Kernstown and Fort Donelson, and when at Shiloh he saw what a field littered with ten thousand dead looked like, he basically lost his mind.

"Do you know what a cannonball does to a line of human beings?" Eisen asked of me. "Bodies upon bodies... piles of bodies... torn to pieces and jumbled together like offal. Like a leviathan sickle had swept through the men and reaped their tasty bits."

He continued to serve, continued to saw off limbs and save what lives he could, but at some point in the spring of '62 he became obsessed with the notion of effecting an end to the war.

"My people didn't have slaves or plantations to protect. All I saw was young men dying in numbers enough to invoke the Apocalypse."

On the evening of June 25, 1862, at the outset of the Seven Days and with Union forces nearly knocking on the city gates, Eisen made his move. A list of troop strengths and positions had fallen into his hands during a meeting with senior officers trying to allot triage units accordingly. His daring but foolish plan was to sneak across to the enemy and personally deliver that information to General McClellan. Eisen knew along with everyone else that if Richmond fell, the entire Confederacy would soon follow. He was captured en route, however, and a search uncovered enough evidence to take him into custody. He did not help matters by trying to convince his captors to join him in treason.

According to Eisen, being sent to Castle Thunder while he awaited trial was a natural progression in his own private *Inferno.* For certain his descriptions of the prison made it sound like nothing less than the ninth circle of hell. I myself had, on more than one occasion, stood outside the imposing old tobacco warehouse on Cary and wondered what sort of fiendish treatment was accorded the low men housed within. I never lingered long, though, for the guards took unkindly to anyone paying too much attention.

Eisen told me that in addition to all the spies, traitors, and prisoners of war, Castle Thunder also housed an invisible population of evil men no other facility cared to contain—soldiers who had, either in the course of their service or in its tormented wake, committed acts heinous enough to revoke their right to due process, and were thereby kept hidden from the attention of the press and the general populace.

"Such as?" I interrupted. God help me, I had to know.

Eisen waved away the question, and then answered it anyway. "Infanticide. Battlefield necrophilia. Trophy collecting of the most revolting sort imaginable."

Eisen called these men 'demons', and it was his belief—which I found credible, given the other despicable charges publicly leveled at Commandant Alexander—that the guards at Castle Thunder used these inhumans as their personal thugs, to enforce rules and deliver punishments. In Eisen's case, they evidently went beyond the pale and became the demonic beings he took them to be.

Everyone in the prison knew that Eisen had served as a field surgeon and what things this meant he had done in the name of medicine. They also knew he had attempted to hand Richmond to the North. Many of his fellow traitors came to him for whatever doctoring he could muster, and Eisen was able to survive while other men starved thanks to their miniscule payments of bread and broth. But a handful of the demons had fallen under the saw, and they did not thank their surgeons but instead blamed them for their whole cursed existence and whatever sins they had committed to get there. Two such fiends, named Blount and Cobham, took a special interest in Eisen, and with help from their cohorts they harassed him mercilessly. Until they bored of petty tortures. One dark night in a fit of bloodlust they descended on Eisen, hung him to within an inch of death, and then cut off his arms and legs.

Eisen delivered this denouement with the same nonchalance exhibited above, and for a moment I thought his whole account was an elaborate dido.

"What do you mean they cut off your arms and legs?"

"Exactly that. The demons understood only the most medieval definition of justice, and so they decreed that for my crimes against king and country I must be drawn and quartered. They stripped me naked and strung me up in the prison basement using a length of the barbed wire that kept us from scaling the fence." Here Eisen paused and displayed the jagged scar I had noticed that night in the bar. "Lacking a horse to drag me around with or a blade to disembowel me, they simply took turns using the barbed wire like a rope saw until I was nothing but a torso lying in a pool of my own blood."

I stared at Eisen a moment, unable to speak, silently beseeching his face for some hint of deception. "And then?"

"And then the guards found me and tossed me into a shallow grave in the potter's field behind the prison."

"And then?"

Eisen looked at me blankly, shrugged, and shook his head. He opened his mouth to speak, inhaled sharply, and then just shook his head again. He had no answer, no explanation. Instead he lifted the sheet from his stump, loosened the belt around the bag of earth, and invited me to look inside.

Old Dominion

The road in was little more than a muddy path salted with just enough shale and fallen branches to keep Hale's battered Jeep from bogging down. Two flanking stone walls marked the property line, but someone with great strength and determination had dislodged and regrouped an impressive number of the stones into a massive cairn that left no room to pass. Hale spent the better part of the afternoon dismantling the obstacle, and by the time he was done his hands were bleeding and he was bathed in sweat. The way beyond led into a grove of old oak and sycamore that towered over the sodden track and canceled the daylight. Inside the Jeep, even the glare of the dash-mounted GPS appeared to dim as a black mass of unmapped terrain inked onto the screen and swallowed the little car icon. Hale smiled, despite what lay on his backseat. For better or worse, he had found his terra incognita.

More accurate to say that it had found him.

Still burning with a toxic, chemical fire of anger and grief he could not control or dampen, he'd sat stiffly in the probate attorney's overheated office. He wasn't paying attention the first time he was told that five hundred acres of land at the foot of the Shenandoah now belonged to him. The second time, he heard but did not understand. How was it possible that Polly owned this much property and he didn't know? Had she known? *Yes*, said the attorney, *she knew*. So why didn't he? This the attorney could not answer. Just another secret, then, like the therapist in Alexandria, and the terminated pregnancy, both only discovered while sorting through her insurance claims. Like the reasons she had….

Well, now Hale had a secret too. Polly's will, what there was of one, was explicit. She wanted a direct cremation. Hale demanded to see proof of it when the attorney informed him. The wording was odd and arcane. *No ceremony can mark my passing. If I fail, do not put me in the earth, or foul my body with preservatives. I must be burned. Leave nothing to find or make frolic.*

Hale knew better than to contest the law with a lawyer, but not everyone was so steadfast or wily. A widower's grief is a powerful thing, made all the more so when backed by five crisp Franklins. The crematorium, as it turned out, was in arrears, the retort in dire need of replacement, and the owner was not a scrupulous man. Once the subject had been broached, and their respective ethics uncorked, the man freely admitted that his side deals usually involved discreet disposal, not illegal release—but who was Hale to quibble? It's not like he was giving her to some deviant to butcher or desecrate. Would the man put her in the backseat for him?

"Sure, sure," the man said. "I can do that." Then, "She hasn't been embalmed," he warned, breathing a little heavy from the exertion. "She won't last long."

Hale promised to bury her soon.

Happy to have her back, Hale talked to her on the long drive. At one point he even reached back and placed a hand on her, stroking her arm through the heavy vinyl of the body bag to emphasize a point, the way he had before—but rigor had passed and there was a softness to her now that kept him from doing it again. He spoke slowly, reasonably, as if trying to convince a child. He simply could not bear to have her gone entirely. There must be a place to visit, somewhere he knew she would be forever. Even if in secret. Even if against her wishes. Surely she must understand. She had taken from him the future he had mapped out for them. He deserved some consideration. The needs of the living must outweigh the demands of the dead.

The tone was familiar and well-practiced. He had used it in the past, to talk her back from the night terrors that too often had taken her, leaving her rigid as driftwood, moaning words her dreambound mouth refused to articulate. He'd used it to gently question her the mornings after, and whenever she'd locked herself in the bathroom, or quit another job. He'd used it every Sunday when he asked her to join him for services at First Fairfax Unitarian, and when she told him she was not fit for a church. He'd used it again in his vain attempt to divest her of the notion. He was proud of his reasonable calm, and the emotional discipline it took to patiently knock on her wall of silence. He thought if only he didn't rush her she would come around eventually and let him in.

It wasn't always like that, of course. Far from it. When she wasn't brooding or paranoid, she lived life as if no heaven awaited her and she must wring maximum enjoyment from each new day before it died. In good moods she savored everything, even the simplest things. A ripe peach, a cup of coffee, vanilla ice cream, even the cheeseburgers he cooked on the little charcoal grill on the little patio of his little townhouse—each bite making her lift her chin and close her eyes, a grin of satisfaction spreading across her face.

As if in rhythm with his thoughts, just as the Jeep entered the tunnel grove, she surprised him by leaking a low moan, hardly audible through the bag and above the thrum of the engine. Hale had heard of such effects—the chemical vestiges of life leaving the body—but still he was startled, and nearly swerved off the road.

"Now you want to talk?" he called back over his shoulder when he had recovered his composure. On those rare occasions when Polly said anything at all about what caused her to live so desperately, she would only assure him he could not possibly understand.

"We all have our crosses to bear, honey. Sharing them lightens the load."

"If you only knew…" was how she would end it.

If only he knew. A most fitting epitaph, for it spoke to more than just the unnamed cause of her troubles, this hidden kingdom in the woods, or the health decision she had made without his input. He also had not known how hard it was to maintain faith in the face of pain and loss. It's so easy to be reasonable and calm when you don't need solace, when everything goes according to plan and life is nothing but a second-hand book of mazes already worked out for you. When Polly died, Hale found himself spinning and dizzy, clueless where to turn or look for a way out.

The Jeep hit a rut and bucked, and she nearly slid off the backseat. He hated to think of her sealed in that bag, collapsing into herself. He wanted to unzip her a little and see her face, but he feared the odor might spoil the moment. He would have to bury her soon, but not before he found the perfect spot. Tomorrow, perhaps. It was still too soon to say goodbye.

Hard to believe they had only met two years ago. Walking in Georgetown, she happened upon his little store, Terra Incognita. She'd misunderstood and came in thinking he sold real, historical maps, made of paper and parchment, not the careful marquetry copies he assembled from pieces of exotic wood veneer. She couldn't hide the disappointment in her face, but she was polite enough to marvel at his craftsmanship and to ask how it was done.

"Little by little," he joked.

Something in his answer kept her lingering, and they talked some more. She had an accent he could not place: southern, sure, but also vaguely foreign and archaic. At the time he guessed she was a lapsed Mennonite, and asked her what sort of map she sought. He closed up early, and they continued talking over dinner in his favorite Mexican joint around the corner. She showed him that appreciative smile after her first taste of chili relleno, and he imagined how lovely it would look above him. They talked for hours, and he got his wish even sooner than expected. But she never explained her interest in old maps.

He was still lost in the memory and driving too fast when he finally emerged from the tunnel grove. The track dipped, and dumped him into even wetter lowland choked with willows and reeds. A sudden bog stretched out on either side of the vehicle, through which snaked a narrow, knobby upthrust of rock like a scoliotic backbone. It was a lucky feature, as otherwise the way forward was impassable and he would have pitched nose-first into the mud. The tires hummed as they skimmed across the wet stone, and he dared not brake lest he swerve and hydroplane. An improbable stone track carrying him across a desolate swamp struck him as something out of the fantasies he'd read as a child, and he wondered at the black knight's errand that had brought him here. The path gradually rose out of the bog and at last became certain and wide enough for him to lift his eyes from the immediate space in front of the hood—and he found another surprise when he did. Atop a small plateau, amidst a scattering of black walnut trees, he saw a little stone house hiding under a curtain of kudzu and creeper.

The lawyer had said nothing of a house.

Hale only planned to bury her someplace nice—somewhere he could revisit in private, whenever he wanted. But a house changed everything. The moment he saw the place, that nihilist feeling of a stolen future started to fade and a whole new possibility rolled out before him like a mural, nearly complete in its particulars. He would close the shop in Georgetown and sell his overpriced condo. He would fix up this house and live out here. He would build a workshop and sell his wooden maps over the internet, making weekly trips to the nearest post office. He would plant a garden and put in a patch of lilies where he buried her, and each spring her favorite flowers would come up and remind him of her smile.

He was so wrapped up in this uncharacteristically maudlin fantasy that he almost didn't notice the furious buzzing that burst from the backseat like a cicada trying to shed its exoskeleton. The oscillations of the old Jeep engine would sometimes cause some item inside the cabin to vibrate and make a shocking racket, so at first he chalked it up to that—but when the buzzing got louder the closer he came to the house, he was forced to admit it was coming from the body bag. By the time he reached a proper place to park, the sound had so unnerved him that he cut the engine, threw open the door, and jumped from the driver's seat as if the vehicle might explode. Standing some distance away, he stared at the back window, eyes squinted and cocked hard aslant, desperately trying to convince himself the fitful movements he saw within were just swaying tree limbs, stirring the reflected glare of the late afternoon light. If not that, then some other cruel effect of decay unknown to him. In time the movements slowed and then ceased altogether and when they did his mind pulled a little sleight of hand by focusing on his new house instead.

Or the strange old house on the land newly his.

In style and make, it was more like something a medieval monk would inhabit than your typical backwoods cabin. For one, it was made of the same mammoth fieldstones used in the property marker walls and the cairn. For another, it was tiny and lacked all niceties and nods to leisure—no sitting porch or swing, no flower boxes or brick walks. The heavy oak door bore a faded mark on its front, a dull red glyph that meant nothing to him. In any case, it was locked and he had no keys, so he looked around back for some means of ingress. He found a creeper-covered window into the kitchen with a crosspiece so rotted and soft that the lock latch ripped clean out when he lifted it. The smell within was old and earthy, as if he had cracked open a cave or root cellar. The window was inordinately small. For a moment he got stuck trying to shimmy inside, and he imagined himself as a hapless skeleton, his body pecked clean by the birds and discovered by the next foolhardy soul to come along. Which got him thinking: *How long had it been since anyone was here?* Polly's mother was dead ten years when they met, and her father had abandoned her when she was still a child. Hale had always assumed this was the basis of her issues. She had no siblings or cousins, at least as far as he knew. All of which helped explain why this Yarrow family plot had passed to him, but gave him no specific answer to his original question aside from saying it had been a long, long time.

Once he'd freed himself and tumbled into the house, the state of things inside certainly seemed to support that notion. A potbellied wood stove shared the kitchen with a narrow pantry cabinet, a freestanding washbasin, and legions of dead insects. That was it. There was no plumbing as far as he could tell. No appliances either: no fridge, no toaster, no coffeemaker. No electrical outlets to support them. Silly to think of electricity running all this way into the woods, but Hale was born and raised in Reston, where nothing standing was older than 1964 and a few acres made a fiefdom. He had wallpapered over that historical void with pages from paperbacks about dragons and sorcerers, and grew up drawing maps to places that did not exist, dreaming in secret of conquering a kingdom of his own and building a place like this. Well, not like this perhaps, but still. The old adage about being careful what you wish for threatened to rise up and laugh at him, but he pushed it down with all the other things he wasn't thinking about.

It took five minutes to tour the rest of the house, and that included tying back the mildewed curtains in each room along the way. The kitchen led into a dining area, with a small oak slab table and several handmade chairs with woven reed seats. In the corner, by the door, was a short-handled rush broom only a bent-backed old hag would use. The eating area led to a great room—if one could even use the term—with a fireplace, a rocking chair, a small pine bed, and a plain pine dresser. Everything was functional. On the far wall of this room hung the only decorative item in the entire house. At first Hale thought it might be a dartboard cabinet, but that was ridiculous, and it looked hundreds of years old. It was a simple yet handsome piece of figured walnut, and incongruous enough to invite a closer look—but after he noticed it, Hale realized it would be dark soon and the temperature was dropping fast. He had a tent and a sleeping bag in the Jeep; there was no good reason not to sleep in the house. He just needed to get his things and gather some wood.

Back outside he was reminded of what 'his things' included. He couldn't leave her there, locked overnight in the backseat like a piece of fruit fallen from a grocery bag. He gave himself no time to think or hesitate. He just opened the back door and hoisted the bag over his shoulder. No movement or sound attended the maneuver, only a small expiration of fetid air through the zipper that forced him to hold his breath as he lugged her inside. He laid her down as gingerly as possible and wondered whether now might be the time to steal a look at her. *No, not yet*, he decided. *Better get prepared for the night.*

There was no shortage of wood, but all of it was fallen branches that would burn hot and fast, so he collected seven armfuls and dumped them in a big pile by the fireplace. With each haul the sun dipped and reddened, tearing the horizon until all that remained was a thin scar between the bruised sky and the bare trees. He stood holding the last load and watched until the color was gone.

There was just enough light left to prepare the fire. Fearing it wouldn't catch without newspaper, he over-kindled. The dry tinder smoked for a while and then exploded, throwing flames high up into the flue. He stood too close, and as the sudden heat warmed his face and body he nearly fell asleep standing up, unaware until then how drained he was from the day's strangeness and rigor. He had not eaten anything since lunch, which didn't help, but he wasn't about to prepare something now. He washed down a granola bar with some water from a thermos, unpacked his sleeping bag, and collapsed onto the bed fully clothed. Fire-born sprites danced on the ceiling and stole the last of his will to stay conscious.

***

Something jerked him from a dream of vague rebuke into an utter and unfamiliar darkness. He blinked and listened, waiting for the sound that woke him to recur or for its memory to manifest more clearly. He did not have to wait very long.

Something was in the room with him. Something large that scuffed the floor in stealthy fits and starts. He sat up and extracted his head from the cowl of his mummy sleeping bag. Cold air poured down his neck as he strained to pick out anything in the blackness. The abandoned fire was long dead, lacking even a hint of embers to see by. In the end his ears were enough, as the whispery scuffling came again and a second, deeper chill sluiced through him as he arrived at a terrible conclusion. Attracted by the smell, some animal must have come to scavenge Polly and was trying to drag her off somewhere more conducive to eating in private. Only two animals native to Virginia were big enough to even attempt such a thing: a bear or a cougar. Despite the unlikelihood of either's entry into the house, let alone the lack of any animal smell or sound, the thought of a large predator trapped in a small space with him sent Hale's boy scout brain into badge-test mode, unpacking old trunks of memory for the proper response. Cower and play dead, or bluff and shout? He was still vacillating between the two when he remembered his flashlight. Thankfully his backpack was on the bed with him and as the thing continued to scuffle, he slowly reached for and extracted the light. What it revealed was far worse than a bear.

The body bag was unattended. And moving on its own. With a dreadful slowness, it bunched and flattened like a black vinyl inchworm until it reached a wall, where it worked itself upright and then paused a moment, as if to rest.

What the hell was happening? It only took a few seconds to run through the options, and all of them were impossible save one: *Polly wasn't dead.*

Hale leapt from the bed, raced over, and unzipped the bag. When he pushed it back to reveal her face, her pale and withered countenance stole his air. He inhaled, and the smell of her marched him across the room and sat him down on his ass. Shuddering from the cold and the shock of it, he struggled to train the light on her face. Something in him severed when she opened her eyes. A thin filament vaporized—the one inside the fuse that buffered his brain from information it could not process, and the failsafe forgetfulness that had protected him that afternoon—giving way to a full and unfiltered awareness.

He watched as her long, white fingers reached up and tugged open the bag wide enough to shrug it off her shoulders. He watched as she rose up, naked and nearly translucent, burnt patches of her still glistening and the flesh sagging earthward with a rank over-ripeness that moiled his empty stomach. He watched as she took her first unsteady step, and then another, the gait clumsy and tottering, as if she were being tugged forward by an unseen force, balancing her hips and leg bones atop each other without aid of muscle or tendon. And all the while she kept her gaze on him, milky eyes wide and chiding.

He continued watching, unable to move, as she lurched towards the door, where she stopped and passed four words through her wasted larynx before her limp hands struggled with the door and she staggered out.

Do not follow me.

***

For a time nothing at all went through his mind. He sat quite still, both motion and emotion stymied by the paradox that kept crashing his consciousness each time he tried to reboot: *Polly was dead; Polly was out there walking in the night.*

Little by little, bits of information surfaced to support each side of this illogical equation, but did nothing to balance it. All the strange and cryptic things she had said to him, the wording of her will, even the manner with which she had tried to end her life—they all presaged this. Hale recalled her difficulty with the alarm system at his condo, her apparent ignorance that such technology even existed. Clearly she had not known about the sprinkler system that saved her from the total immolation she desired while failing to keep her lungs clear of the smoke that finally killed her.

As frightened as he was, he gave no thought to leaving. For one, he was inescapably culpable. By defying her last wishes, he had realized her worst fears. For another, those four parting words had only achieved an opposite effect. They proved that something of her remained. And whatever that something was, he owed it help and, if possible, salvation. At that thought, his inertia finally evaporated. He rose and waved the light around the room in search of some weapon or tool to give him enough courage to get out there after her. During the sweep, his light landed on the odd decorative piece in the corner that had grabbed his attention earlier. Now that he was upright and moving again, every instinct told him not to delay—that each moment wasted was one in which he continued to fail her. Something about that hanging cabinet transfixed him, and he walked over to examine it. It was too small for rifles or shotguns, but if he was lucky it might contain something old and strong and sharp. A simple iron catch held it closed. Once lifted, two stacked leaves opened up and away from a central panel on heavy hinges. Revealed inside was a triptych of painted woodcuts. They were carved with hacks and gouges—clearly the work of a child—and yet obviously meant to function as some sort of primer. The only colors used were a dull red and a deep granular black, the pigments too crude and organic to be anything but dried blood and bone char. Terrible enough, beneath the harsh glare of the flashlight, but it was the subject matter that truly disturbed him.

The left panel showed a trio of wagons moving through a wood. In the ground beneath the wagons was a tall, twisted thing surrounded by wormy squiggles and scattered pieces of stick people. In the central panel, the twisted figure was standing at the head of a wide clearing, ropey arms spread wide. A group of people lay before it, all dead or prostrate save two: a bearded burly man, nearly as large as the twisted thing, leaning over a cane and holding aloft the hand of a little one with long hair. The last panel showed two scenes: on one side was a tight grouping of cabins, with chevrons of hearth smoke rising from their chimneys and smiling stick families standing in front. On the other, a small house stood all by itself in a thick wood. Nearby, in a small clearing ringed with gnarled shapes, the twisted thing and the little girl were entwined on the ground, their limbs jumbled and the girl's head turned away.

***

Hale followed her as closely as he dared. He tried to keep quiet, but lugging a nearly full can of gas made it almost impossible to move gingerly, and dead leaves crackled underfoot with each hitching step. Upon leaving the house, he manically scanned the lower ground in all directions and saw nothing but the circles of crosshatching limbs lit up by the flashlight. A half-moon had risen while he slept, and he realized that he could see without the flashlight. It was only when he cut the switch and stopped moving that he picked up the sounds of her lurching through the forest. Zeroing in took a few moments more, but once he did, he caught a glimpse of white skin between two trees. She was still moving with that dreadful gait, like something dragging shackles. Her plodding pace gave him a moment to breathe and allowed him to remember the gas can. He always kept it on hand for emergencies, but it was usually empty. A quick map search before leaving Reston had warned him how few and far between filling stations would be out here, and he wondered—as he snatched it from the trunk and tore off after her—where the Jeep's gauge now sat. He had filled up halfway, but all those snaking country roads ate up a lot of mileage.

On the hill down below, he saw another flash of white and heard the crunch as she pitched forward and fell. She must have laid there a spell, because he lost sight of her in the underbrush. At that point he probably could have closed most of the distance between them, but as he was maneuvering to regain a vantage point a rush of terror swept through his body. He dropped to a crouch without thinking, and remained absolutely still. His eyes widened and then bulged as he began to sense the other things moving all around him. He could not hear them at all, or see anything but the dimmest outlines of their shadowy forms, but he could certainly *feel* them. They were human in shape and size, but lacked all substance and seemed to flicker in and out of being. He could only detect them at all because of the way his body was reacting to their presence, and the slight distortion they inflicted on the space they inhabited, like the air above a stretch of hot tarmac, or his little Weber grill. Something about the softness of their borders, and their gentle bearing suggested the feminine. They weren't stalking Polly so much as searching for her, spread at arm's length and moving as one through the trees with a slow but steady urgency. The way a family might if a child was lost in the woods. That sense was confirmed when two of them reached where Polly had fallen and seemed to gather her up and help her rise. They waited until the others reached them and then they moved together down the hill. Hale let them get a bigger lead on him, and then he stood again and followed.

At the base of the hill, the land flattened out and the trees thinned. Polly and her specter escort shambled on a ways, until they reached a small clearing defended by a dense border guard of desiccated thornbushes. They took no notice and plowed on through, leaving strips of Polly's skin behind. Once inside the clearing they spread out into a circle and assumed the stance of dancers waiting for the music to start. For the specters this was but an abstract impression, a shadow play on the backdrop of the forest, but when Polly tried to gather herself into a graceful posture, her broken-toy body wouldn't cooperate, and for a moment Hale had to look away.

When he looked back the dance had begun.

They circled the clearing at a dirge pace and lifted their wandering palms to the night. Without any conscious decision, Hale began to circle with them, but instead of mimicking their convoluted hand gestures he tipped his can to prime the thorny tangle that enclosed them. When their pace quickened, he quickened his own, and when the air took on the feeling of an approaching storm, without any hint of wind or moisture, and when in the center of their circle a darkness gathered and thickened and the sharp loamy scent of fertile earth and decay filled his nose, he reached into his breast pocket and struck a match, setting fire to the circle. And then he ran for his life.

He could not tell whether the dilating hiss that pursued him was made by the fire itself or the things it threatened. He only wanted to get far from both as fast as possible. Running uphill with the can, even half full, was incredibly awkward and tiring, and as he leaned over to counterbalance its weight, he felt the flashlight shift and fall from his pants pocket. He stopped and turned, as much to catch his breath as to find it. Groping through the leaves with a desperation that bordered on hysteria, he might have laughed at himself if not for the chaos he had wrought down below. The ring of fire had both expanded and constricted, and the specters were backlit and writhing as it closed in. Polly was on her knees, fully engulfed, and though he could not pick out her face from the flames, she wasn't fighting to escape and showed no signs of feeling any pain. Not so for the twisted, tree-sized thing they had summoned. It stalked the contracting circle on four giant, many-jointed legs and its rotting face seethed and mutely bellowed like something watching its children slaughtered. It jutted its misshapen head at him as if to mark him for what he had done. Then it sucked back into the earth that had birthed it and reemerged on the near side of the fire, stalking up the hill after him with great, terrible strides and an aspect so menacing it vaporized all thought of retreat and rooted Hale to his spot. When it was nearly upon him, and it spooled out its terrible limbs, his mind went limp like a rabbit in the mouth of a dog.

***

The smoldering ash pile spat and sizzled as light rain began to fall. Hale remained on the hill where he had dropped the flashlight, bodily unharmed but still in shock and unable to convince himself it was over. Just before the twisted thing took him, Polly's body must have burned enough to cleave their connection and revoke the demon's claim to the physical world. It collapsed at his feet and disassembled into a squirming mass of saprophagous insects and annelids that quickly burrowed out of sight. Hale was left to wonder what that meant, and whether the contract Polly's ancestors had made with it was now broken or void—and if broken, what new dominion it might seek to find the human carrion that invoked and sustained it.

When he finally rose—sodden, freezing and exhausted—his legs were stiff and bloodless and it seemed to take forever to climb the rest of the hill. A sad, pale dawn broke along the way. When he checked the Jeep, he found it had just enough fuel. He could use what was left in the can to burn the house, or at least its wooden infrastructure. He ripped the heinous triptych from the wall and piled his unburned kindling on top. He doused the room with the gas and lit his third and final fire. He lingered long enough to dry the chill from his body, and then he drove away with the orange glow flickering in his rearview mirror, and black smoke rising into the gray sky.

The drizzle turned into a downpour as he slowly made his way out, and when he arrived at the quaggy lowland he found the bridge of rock nearly submerged. No sane man would have attempted it, but he could not lay claim to that title anymore, and he squeezed the wheel and skated across the swamp with a grim resolve that most would mistake as suicidal.

At the stone walls he got out and rebuilt the cairn in the rain, and several times he stumbled and collapsed into the mud under the weight of the field stones. When he was finished it was neither as tall nor as wide as its predecessor, but he draped the body bag over the top and weighed it down with a few more stones. And trusted its meaning was clear.

Bone Black

Lorraine was fine. *No, really*, she'd say, if anyone asked. She put all the time alone to good use, rewriting a thorny chapter on the celestial imagery of Keats's *Endymion*. The poem's melancholic glories left her oddly refreshed and hopeful about actually finishing her dissertation.

If only. If only, *in spite of all, some shape of beauty would move away the pall from her dark spirit*. But no one did ask and so she wasn't forced to lie. Thrust away by her fixation on Sam, the few friends who belonged to her and truly warranted the designation were all orbiting at icy apogee. The rest of them were Sam's friends, and had likely abandoned her tiny corner of the social universe forever. Cut off from any human interaction, she barely left the couch, spending whole days staring at the space where his smart TV used to sit and surviving on expired tins of tuna and ossified Saltines. It was nothing like a triumph of will that eventually forced her out of hiding, but rather a hopeless addiction to wholewheat toast.

Taking the smart TV (and the Netflix/Hulu/HBO accounts) had been cruel enough—he could afford all that and knew damn well that she could not—but in his final act of spite, Sam had also taken with him the only thing that *really* mattered to Lorraine in the entire apartment. Sure, his parents were the original owners, and sure, he had lugged it around for over a decade in an uncharacteristic nod to nostalgia, but that toaster *belonged* to her. Sam would happily eat toast of any shade or stripe: under-browned, over-buttered, soggy, bipolar, or burnt to ash. To him, toast was just an edible shovel, or something to dip into his soup. It had no value on its own.

She, on the other hand, was a toast connoisseur of the highest order. Plain wholewheat toast constituted an inordinately large percentage of her diet, and she had come to require a very specific degree of crisping. In her opinion, there was one and only one infinitesimal half-step in the Maillard reaction that produced the perfect marriage of give and crunch, wheat and carbon. To her it was axiomatic that properly toasted bread could stand on its own, without need of any fatty veneers or sugary dressings. She had searched all her life for a toaster that could deliver this miracle by default. During her undergraduate years she had auditioned dozens of used models, from every flea market and Goodwill store in town. For a short period of infinite frustration, she even managed to swallow her prized senses of thrift and style and fished for the answer among the brushed stainless decadence of several new toaster ovens. But she always found that their heating coils were spaced too far apart, and the margin of error too large within the empty promise of their calibration dials. No matter what flag was flown by these changeling appliances, they belonged to the tribe of ovens, not toasters. In any case, toaster ovens took up way too much of her limited counter space.

In the end, she had resigned herself to the sad truth that it was asking too much for a machine to achieve this artistry on its own, and had settled for standing watch over a long line of imperfect models, egg timer in hand and forever poised to prematurely jerk up the plunger when that brief moment of perfection arrived. This gave her an acceptable facsimile of the outcome she desired, but also resulted in incremental wear and tear on the timing mechanism and an inevitable breakdown. Eat, toast, repeat. By the time she turned twenty-two she had already begun to lose her religion and ask herself whether all the effort was really worth it. Maybe she should just switch to rice cakes.

Then she met Sam.

To paraphrase his favorite philosopher (did he know of any other?), their courtship was nasty, brutish and short. Sam was decent looking, educated, and most of the time he remembered to brush his teeth. In other words, barely sufficient. Lorraine was tired of being alone, and more than willing to compromise whatever standards and morals she had inherited from her picky, overprotective mother in exchange for regular companionship. Sam was happy to play his part in that transaction. He was a late bloomer, a bit of math nerd, and the first available promise of regular sex was more than enough motivation to coerce him into cohabitation. Halving his overhead didn't hurt.

When Lorraine discovered her Holy Grail amid the boxes and boxes of useless boy crap that Sam brought with him during the move-in, she marked it as a vindication of her relaxed chastity and a clear sign from the gods of serendipity. Here at last was the man she would marry, and with him came the lifelong promise of perfect toast. She enjoyed nearly two years of such rarified bliss. Two years no less perfect for their failure to deliver her a diamond token of his fidelity. It gave them the chance to be young and together without worrying about the next step. Those two years saw Sam graduate with an MBA while she puttered away at a dead-end doctorate in English Literature. When Sam landed a good job, and started going out with a new set of friends, she habitually begged off and stayed behind. What did she need of dancing or trendy drinks when she had her Romantic Poets and little slices of heaven? She never worried about him straying, because he always came home and her toast always came out perfect. Surely the toaster would warn her if things were getting stale. Even when he sheepishly asked her if she had ever thought about sharing him with another woman, she just chalked it up to harmless fantasy. Besides, the job was asking a lot of him, with all those business trips, and if he needed to blow off steam with a little dirty talk, that was okay with her. Was it really all that different from her trysts with Shelley in the bathtub?

By the time she wised up enough to recognize the signs of its disintegration, their relationship was already over. Sam came back to her for a brief time after she threatened to do terrible things, but once the crisis passed, he paid her rent for six months, made arrangements for a psychiatrist friend to check on her, and then severed ties altogether. She wouldn't need the psychiatrist if he left the goddamn toaster and the smart TV. But he hadn't, and so here she was, readying herself to venture forth and quest after another.

Fearing she only had the energy for one such errand, she had scanned Craigslist on her laptop all morning for mention of toasters and televisions, only checking the free listings as an afterthought when the Electronics and Household Appliance sections failed to yield results. Nothing recent fit the bill, but a curb alert posted nearly a week ago promised to contain both items and a whole lot more. The street mentioned sounded familiar for some reason, but Lorraine didn't dally trying to figure out why. Instead she grabbed her keys and ran out the door without bothering to change her clothes or fix her hair. For all she knew, a trash truck might be arriving that very moment to take away her new toaster.

It was all still there when she arrived in her geriatric Subaru. What looked to be the entire contents of a small house was stacked indiscriminately on the sidewalk in front, leaving barely enough room for pedestrians to pass. Lorraine immediately wondered how that much had remained unclaimed. The neighborhood was very blue collar—not so proud that its denizens would turn up their noses at free stuff. She parked the car in front and found her answer in the cordon of yellow police tape that had once wrapped the building and now lay in torn sections on the dead lawn. Seeing the tape triggered the hazy memory of a news report, numbly watched while Sam paced the room and apologized. Someone had died here. Not just some*one*, and not just *died*—an entire family had been murdered by their Hungarian au pair. With a knitting needle? Yep, that's right, with a knitting needle. At the time, in the throes of hysterical self-pity, Lorraine could only interpret this half-heard report as tacit support for the hot flashes of homicidal intent that boiled behind her eyes while Sam stammered and dissembled.

Now, standing in front of this sad little house, with its contents splayed helter-skelter on the sidewalk like some kind of modern art installation, she felt only a small measure of relative good fortune. Her life might be a hot mess right now, but at least she had one. On the heels of that thought came the dirty shame of rifling through the possessions of the dead, like some sort of graverobber. But was all this stuff really better off in a landfill? Perhaps by saving a few items, and giving them new life, she could somehow honor the victims' memory. Thus armed with a serviceable rationalization, she began sifting through the piles in search of the toaster.

She found the television first. It was not flat, it weighed a ton, and she had no idea whether it worked or not. But it would have to do. She loaded it into her trunk, grunting the whole while under the strain. She was returning to the pile when she noticed the silence.

When she pulled up, a man was mowing his lawn several houses down, and four kids were loudly waging a street hockey war in a nearby driveway. All of them were now frozen in place, watching her. Additional onlookers seemed to appear in several sets of windows. She couldn't be sure what she saw in their faces—animosity, fear, judgment, morbid fascination?—but it definitely felt like she was in the middle of an unspoken moral standoff. Clearly she was crossing a line that no one else had yet dared to cross. But instead of backing down or thinking too much about it, Lorraine stared back at them. She could never have verbalized why, but standing her ground and asserting her right to happiness suddenly became terribly important. Maybe the most important thing she would ever do. This game of psychic chicken seemed to go on for ages, but in reality lasted all of ten long seconds. The guy at the lawnmower gave up first, and the others quickly followed suit. The world regained its sense of normalcy and Lorraine returned to her quest for the toaster.

She was waylaid en route by an odd little painting, found face down inside a gray file cabinet. No more than a foot tall by eight inches wide, the canvas was entirely covered from border to border with a chunky layer of the darkest, truest black she had ever seen. The pigment had been applied with chaotic abandon, so it wasn't easy to tell for sure, but it seemed to Lorraine that something was hiding amid all the random swirls and brushstrokes. The longer Lorraine looked at it, the more certain she became. She let her eyes drift in and out of focus. Yes. Definitely a person. Yes. A young girl. Yes. Emerging from the black. *Yes.* Her body was merely suggested, and the head just a cursory half-moon, but enough of her mouth and eyes was present to give her a beguiling look of complete inscrutability. A certain lean of her head, the way her neck and shoulders twisted, gave the impression that she was regarding the viewer with… what? Well, to Lorraine the face suggested the same dark jumble of emotions that she had just fought off from the peanut gallery.

Given her chosen discipline, Lorraine was steeped enough in the pitfalls of subjective interpretation to know that any successful work of art wielded an almost quantum power to change state, form, and direction in relation to its observer. She also knew that she was not quite right in her head. Nonetheless she felt an instant connection with the painting; one so inexorable and overwhelming that she would have sworn up and down to anybody who would listen that the hidden girl was *looking at her.* It was not a distressing feeling, exactly, just strange and somehow wondrous. Without a moment's hesitation she placed the painting in her passenger seat and went back for the toaster, which, as it turned out, had been sitting all along in full view, on the arm of a futon couch. It was just the right kind: heavy and aluminum, and built to last. She had no idea how she had missed it before, but was glad she had not found it too soon.

In the car on the way back Lorraine kept stealing glances at the painting. She felt lucky and elated. Amazing how little it takes to change one's mood. The television and even the toaster were temporarily forgotten in her rush to take the painting upstairs and find it a home. She picked a spot in the living room, above the couch, that was visible from both the kitchen and the little niche in between what she jokingly called her office. That way, in idle moments at the stove or at her desk, she could always gaze at the girl and find solace in their shared looks of pained confusion.

Riding her recovery, Lorraine decided to give someone a call. She thought of Molly first, but then she remembered Molly was also suffering from post-traumatic breakup syndrome and the last thing she needed was a wallow session, so she settled on Robyn instead. He was a better choice anyway: big and strong enough to help her get the TV upstairs, queer and funny (so bound to bring some levity to the situation), but most importantly he was a post-doc in art conservation and would surely appreciate her new painting. Robyn made it clear on the phone that he was still pissed at her for refusing his sympathy invite to that Penis Panic show, but he hated to eat alone and had a weakness for risotto, so it wasn't all that hard to convince him to come over.

"Kind of a grim souvenir, don't you think?"

They were sharing a bottle of wine, staring at the painting while the risotto cooked. Lorraine had filled him in on the back story.

"Why do you say that?"

Robyn clenched his face and threw his eyes sideways.

"You're a strange bird, Lorraine."

She shrugged off his assessment. "Isn't the black outrageous?"

"It ought to be. It's bone black." Robyn's voice dropped nearly an octave, as it always did when a topic fell into his wheelhouse.

Instead of asking outright, Lorraine just raised her eyebrows at him and waited.

"It's a specific kind of black pigment. Made with burnt animal bones."

She waited a few beats for the laugh line, but it never came. "You're serious."

Robyn nodded.

"How can you tell?"

"Neutron Activation Autoradiography."

"Oh come on, Robyn. Knock it off."

"I am dead serious, Lorraine." For a second, his normal voice was back. Then he regained his gravitas. "It's a conservation technique that's been around since the late '60s. I actually joint-taught a short course on it with a cute genius in the physics department. We had to borrow their reactor."

Lorraine still wasn't buying it. Robyn was a known prankster who liked to prey on people's ignorance. "And you got too close to the reactor and now you have neutron eyeballs?"

"No, *wisenheimer*, I spent so much time looking at samples that I can spot bone black from a hundred yards. It's not like it's rare. Rembrandt used it like it was going out of style, but his stuff was made with ivory, long before there were laws against such things. This pigment is…" Robyn stepped closer and nearly touched his nose to the canvas, "really chunky and impure. As if the maker really didn't know what they were doing." Then he asked, out of nowhere: "Was it hers or theirs?"

"What do you mean?"

"The painting. Did it belong to the family or the au pair?"

Odd in retrospect, but the question had never occurred to her. She just assumed it was all the family's stuff. "I don't know. Wouldn't the au pair's stuff still be caught up in legal red tape?"

"Maybe. If she were still alive."

Lorraine punched him in the arm. His little spook story had gone on long enough.

For his part, Robyn just grabbed his shoulder and looked wounded. "Where have you been? It was all over the news. And don't punch me."

"I didn't have a TV, you big jerk, or have you already forgotten about the boat anchor you lugged up here."

They both glared at the object in question, which had powered on for a brief glorious moment before flaring out in a literal blaze of glory that left an acrid smell lingering in its wake.

"Ever hear of the internet?"

"Unlike some people I know, I don't surf the web for true crime tragedies."

"No… you just use it to pickpocket dead people."

The comeback hurt, but only for a moment. Robyn was smiling when he said it, and then Lorraine was distracted by the smell of burnt risotto.

A delivery pizza and another bottle of wine later, there were tears on the couch, and Robyn put his arms around her and tried his best to make her laugh. When that didn't work, they just sat for a while in silence. Eventually, Robyn let go of her, leaned forward, and put his hands on his thighs, as if he was about to beg off.

"So what happened to her anyway?" Lorraine said, to keep him from leaving.

"Who?"

"What's her name… the knitting needle girl."

"Her name was Murin." Robyn paused a moment and tilted his head at that detail, as if it gave him an idea. It must have been a good one, because he failed to answer her question.

"Okay… what happened to Murin?"

"Murin was her last name." Robyn was still off in idea-land and responded slowly, without looking at her. "She managed to steal a pen when they were booking her, and she jammed it into her eye. When that didn't quite finish the job, she wedged it into the table somehow and slammed her head down onto it." He mimed the action like a woodpecker. And then, without much pause, "Hey, would you mind if I took a sample of this?" He threw a thumb upwards at the painting, which hung over their heads. "I have a group of undergrads coming into the lab on Monday and I can use it as a case study."

"They let undergrads use the reactor?"

"No, of course not. Time on that thing is scarce. We're going to old-school it… centrifuge and mass spectrometer."

"Okay, I guess. But do you have to take it with you?" Despite everything that Robyn had told her, she really didn't want to let the girl out of her sight.

"Not necessarily. Got any empty aspirin bottles?"

Robyn used an emery board to file away at a tiny section in the corner and collected the resulting dust in the little plastic pill bottle, which he had carefully washed and dried beforehand. When he was finished, Lorraine could tell he was really itching to bail.

"You're free to go," she said, patting his arm. "Sorry I punched you. And thanks for cheering me up."

Robyn narrowed his eyes and gave her another dubious look. Then he turned to go. "Strange bird…" he sang up to her as he descended the stairs.

***

That night Lorraine dreamed of the girl in the painting. She was sitting on the edge of Lorraine's bed in a pose that mirrored her stance in the painting. There was something deeply wrong with her. Lorraine kept trying to look around at the other side of her face, but there was nothing to see. She had been halved up the middle.

"Do you like toast?" Lorraine found herself asking.

The girl nodded shyly.

"Me too."

***

She was still thinking about the dream the next morning while she stood at the kitchen counter, staring at the girl and waiting to see if the scavenged toaster worked. She always gave them a first chance to do it right, without any intervention. She exhaled long and loud when the bread popped up a little burnt. Entirely inedible.

"Back to the drawing board," she sighed.

The girl stared back her with that pitiful look of hurt. Or was it anger?

"Not you, silly," Lorraine laughed. Now the girl wasn't angry. Not at Lorraine, anyway.

***

She dreamed of the girl again that night, but in this dream she *was* the girl, among a bunch of people at a party. She walked around, awkwardly trying to hide her deficiency, but no one seemed to notice her missing half. Sam and Robyn were there as well, and there was also a guy who was supposed to be Keats but he looked more like John Cusack. Robyn kept telling her to recover the grail, but Keats/John Cusack cut in and argued that the grail motif was all wrong for her. *Screw all that virtuous bullshit,* he said. What she needed was a metaphor of transformation. Something like a crucible to fire-harden the parts of her that were too soft and to liquefy everything else so that she might be remade in the mold of a more perfect vessel.

Like toast? she asked, and Keats/John Cusack just stared back her, not understanding.

Sam chuckled from across the room, and gave her a haughty, withering look that energized a red hot coil of rage inside her belly.

She awoke still angry, under too many blankets, sporting a terrible hangover. The girl was staring back at her from across the room. Lorraine didn't remember moving her to the bedroom, but couldn't discount it either. The indulgence with Robyn had kicked off a two-day wine binge and she wasn't exactly famous for a high alcohol tolerance. Her head felt like the victim of a blind acupuncturist.

The thought inadvertently flooded her mind with a vision of the au pair stabbing out the light in her charge's eyes with a knitting needle. Until that point, she had managed to keep her brain from going there. The images were so vivid, so photographic, that she wondered for a moment whether she *had* seen the crime photos.

She felt a presence in the room—someone sitting on the edge of her bed. She shook her head, trying to snap out of it, but only managed to set off a supernova of pain behind her temples. She wasn't prone to migraines and couldn't be sure if she had ever had one, but surely nothing could be worse than this. She closed her eyes again and curled into a ball to stop her head from spinning. The position only worsened her vertigo. She felt like she was floating on the ceiling, looking down at herself. From this new vantage, her coiled and lumpy bedsheets looked very much like the swirling texture of the painting. Desperate for relief, she dove headlong into that offered oblivion.

Sometime later she found herself standing in the kitchen, readying herself to leave. On the way out she saw that she had replaced the painting above the couch. Now she saw something like equanimity in the girl's face. Perhaps even approval.

Her cell phone rang in her purse as she was heading out the door, but she had her car keys in one hand and the heavy old toaster in the other, and decided to let it ring. A few seconds later, her landline rang. She decided the machine could get it, but she would wait a second to see who it was.

"Pick up Lorraine. It's important." Robyn's serious teacher voice sounded even deeper than usual. He paused, hoping she would comply.

Lorraine looked at the girl, and decided not to.

"Okay, but call me when you get this… I think you should take that painting to the police. The pigment has human DNA in it. I trust you understand what that means. Crazy as it sounds, I think I might know who made it. There was this insane Hungarian painter in the '80s who hacked up his young wife and used her bones—"

Something cut him off midsentence. It was Lorraine's finger on the kill button. She was already in a hurry and now she needed to add another errand to her list.

If she had any thoughts or sensations during the drive, her memory kept no record of them. The next she knew she was standing in the hallway outside of Sam's new apartment. She heard water running inside and stabbed the doorbell nearly two dozen times at regular intervals until he finally came to the door wearing a towel and a disgruntled look.

"What are you doing here?"

"I need my toaster. You can have this one."

Her voice was calm, even casual. Sam looked down at the heavy metal thing in her hands. A dented corner was covered in blood and chunks of pinkish gray.

"It's not your toaster," Sam said weakly, involuntarily retreating into his apartment.

Lorraine used the opportunity to step inside. "I know." She shut the door behind her and began to coil the toaster's electrical wire around one hand, "But I need it."

"How did you know where I live?"

"You told me, silly. So I could forward your mail."

She let the toaster drop and dangle at the end of its tether like a morning star. Sam backed up even further and raised his hands in a gesture of surrender, causing his towel to drop. He looked down at his nakedness long enough for Lorraine to swing the toaster up into his groin. A whoosh of air and a guttural groan escaped him and he doubled over. Lorraine yanked the toaster backwards, reversing its rotation, and swung it around in a hissing arc that halved Sam's overhead forever. She punctuated the act with several more just like it. Then she went to the kitchen, swapped out the bludgeon for her crucible, and readied herself for what came next. Water was still running in the bathroom down the hall. It made her realize how much she needed a bath.

***

Molly felt terrible about sorting through her dead friend's bookcase, but she really wanted her copy of Baudelaire's *Les Fleurs du mal* back, and this might be her only chance to retrieve it. Lorraine's mother stood leaning against the wall, staring off into space and smoking a cigarette. They had exchanged a few words at the funeral, and Molly was pained to see how much she suffered, how alone she seemed in her grief. Loneliness and grief were things Molly knew well, so perhaps they could help each other.

"I don't suppose you want that too?" Lorraine's mother jutted her chin at the small painting on the wall. "It gives me the creeps."

Molly's knees popped as she stood to have a closer look. She had spent lots of time in Lorraine's apartment, and couldn't recall ever seeing it before. The small canvas was covered with a thick, swirling layer of very black paint and nothing else, but it seemed to

110

Molly that somewhere amid the swirls and slashing brushstrokes, something was struggling against the constraints of its two-dimensional prison. The painting throbbed, almost vibrated off the wall with the violent beating of its bone-black heart. Molly saw hurt. Anger. Betrayal. But beneath and beyond all that was an immutable longing, the enduring need for rectification. Inchoate. Impatient. And begging to be born.

THE EDEN HOLLOW EVICTIONS

I'm certain it wasn't on the porch when I let Jasper out that morning, only when I let the fickle beast back in a few minutes later. I'd heard no one come up to the house, and the postman wasn't due until much later. I remember feeling a bit silly, getting that unsettled by something as common as an unseen delivery. Then I got a better look at it.

The old mailer was bleached of color and bloated as a well-fed tick. All four of its seams had been sloppily repaired with brittle strands of tape. My name was written on its face, but there was no address or return information. Beneath my name, in a crazed red scrawl:

ENJOY YOUR EVICTION ☺

Handling it felt icky, in the way of ratty old dollars greased with too many dead skin cells. I nearly tossed it unopened, but of course it made me curious. When I cut through one of its taped mouths it exhaled and dribbled some of its insides onto my kitchen table.

On top was an old Polaroid cartridge. Spent and re-used to store three developed photographs. All three seemed to depict the same view—a fallow field and a line of peeling river birch some twenty or thirty yards distant. The focus was soft, the colors muted, but the scene felt familiar. Likely because I had been there so recently. I was reminded of the tree line behind the back field at Eden Hollow, before the land drops down into its namesake ravine.

In the first and second photo, the trees had leaves. In the third, the trees were bare. The third was skewed and blurred enough to suggest it was taken while the photographer was running. Either toward the intended subject—in haste to capture it—or in equally panicked retreat. Several trees were wrapped with thick, hairy vines of poison ivy. The spaces between them were spiked with the desiccated ribs of burweed and underfed volunteers. Hiding within these hostile tangles was a murky stack of ovals, as one might use to start to sketch a human.

From a real estate standpoint, there is nothing remarkable about Eden Hollow. The front ten acres hide in plain sight; just another green stretch of nothing noticeable between two hilly tracts of grazing land. There's no mailbox and no sign of a house from the road. The only way in is a dirt track that is nearly invisible in summer. After a hundred yards or so, opposing stretches of a cattle fence meet at an old gate with a few stubborn flecks of red paint on it. Beyond that lie fifty-two more acres, a good chunk of them covered with mature hardwoods. It was these trees that first attracted my interest during a targeted Google Earth scan of local stands on private land. Rehabbing and flipping old houses was my usual gig, but with the lumber market being what it is, a big stand of hardwood seemed like a good investment.

Beneath the Polaroid cartridge was a piece of old paper inside a dirty sleeve of plastic. The writing was faded and cursive, but relatively neat and legible under bright light.

Robert found Constance today eyes squeezed shut and screaming at the bottom of the holler. Toted her up the hill like that, fighting and flailing at him the whole way. She calmed down a little after sitting with us by the fire, but she still shakes with a palsy that no pile of blankets can still. Her eyes look like a mouse when its back's been broke by a trap. Least she quit with the moaning. Hasn't carried on like that since she was just a little thing and thought she saw something looking up her from the privy pit. She was always such a wiry child, strong for her size. Now she feels soft. Even her bones have some give to them. Smells bad too. Like a wound that won't heal right.

Robert went back down there to scout around and came back after dark, two shells lighter but with no good explanation for why. I seen my husband square off and put down a catamount coming straight for him. I seen him gently hush a horse so spooked its eyes weren't nothing but white. Seeing that man that scared told me plain it was time we pack up and settle somewhere else.

"Sumpin' still down there," was what he said when I demanded an answer. "Couldn't find it but I heard it calling for me in the dark."

Robert has the imagination of a grindstone, so I knew he wasn't telling tales.

"Said your name?" I asked him.

"Not exactly," he said. "I think it was calling me Papa."

The next few things I fished from the pile were all excerpts from scholarly papers, photocopied and folded into thirds. Most were published this century, but little seemed to unite their subject matter. There were articles on alternative stem cell splicing, on Vanishing Twin Syndrome, and on a species of fungus called *Armillaria ostoyae*. Another impenetrable jungle of words on a rare psychiatric disorder known as the 'Capgras Delusion'. I'm not a dumb man, I don't think, but at that point I was not yet savvy enough to tie together those thumbtacks with string.

***

Prior to today, I have been to Eden Hollow only twice. Once before bidding at the auction house, and once following my exposure to what came in the envelope. On both occasions I encountered Jim Routledge, the former owner.

At our first meeting, I found his old Ford parked in front of the gate. The county commissioner warned me about him after he tried to halt the auction with a pointless lawsuit. So I wasn't especially surprised to find him there, just mystified by how he'd learned the timing of my visit.

Squared off like dogs, we both hopped out of our pickups and had some words. I told him he was trespassing. Routledge begged to differ. Also begged me to leave. Actually stalked over and grabbed me by my shirt collar, his mouth too close and smelling of rotten fruit.

I shrugged out of his grip and backed away.

"Why didn't you sell the timber?" I asked. "Enough there for the taxes and then some."

"The trees are long gone," he said nonsensically. "Down its demon gullet."

His accompanying hand gesture seemed to encompass not just this property but the entire world. "You better back away, boy, before it swallows you too."

I don't take kindly to being called 'boy'. And besides, it takes *way* more than that to scare me off. Country folk can be a bit loony about land. I've had perfectly sound buildings burned to the ground, dead skunks hung from doorknobs, toilets clogged with fish heads, copperheads left in mailboxes. It's enough to make you lose your faith in humanity. But not enough to spook me away from a good deal.

I went back to my truck and retrieved the paperwork that granted me the right to look around. I asked Routledge to move his old Ford. He spoke vaguely of some documents he wanted to show me. Things that would convince me I was making a grave mistake. I told him I did my own inspections, thank you, and again demanded he vacate. Routledge refused a third time, so I pretended to call the police. That worked. When I turned around his truck was creeping back down the road.

Nothing weird happened that first visit. I had a thorough look around, but never went further into the ravine than was necessary to measure the diameters of a few trees. The house was a failing mess of ad-hoc additions, dangerous in places and way out of code everywhere else. The outbuildings were even worse, whipperjawed and thick with wasps. The well tested pretty high in coliform bacteria, which isn't that unusual. A shock chlorination should have handled that. The soil sample from the sunniest field was another story. Results came back with very low pH and abnormally high salinity. The lab tech said it was the highest he'd ever seen—almost like someone had intentionally salted the whole place. Out of protection or punishment was anybody's guess. Without an expensive amount of soil amendments, most anything planted there anytime soon would yellow and die. But the trees seemed healthy enough, and these days there are plenty of rural buyers who care nothing for farming or husbandry. Good light, tons of space, some nice high ground for a new country manor, far enough but not too far from town. Even if it never housed another human, the hardwoods alone were worth three times the asking price. Right place, right time, I figured. No one else even bid. I actually giggled a little when the gavel dropped.

***

I can't even recall the last time I'd seen a microcassette. Something was written on the small gatefold inside its plastic case:

PROPERTY OF CUMBERLAND COUNTY POLICE.

Neatly folded and tucked beneath the tape itself was a newspaper clipping about the Gantry boy's disappearance. Jason Gantry was fifteen years old wen he went into the woods behind Eden Hollow in the spring of 1989. Two weeks later he reappeared on the back porch of his own house thirty-seven miles away. He was malnourished and had amnesia, but seemed otherwise unharmed.

Multiple searches were conducted by teams of volunteers over the course of those two weeks. Several locals were interviewed and quoted in the story, and one of them claimed it was impossible for Jason to have been in those woods that whole time without being found. Eden Hollow just wasn't big enough. An abandoned kidnapping was one hypothesis. Others suggested a hoax; some kind of stunt for attention or sympathy. Jason himself said he couldn't remember what happened. His mother described empty eyes and a permanent listlessness following his return. He seemed unable to reply unless coached with a suitable response. He never returned to school, and he never returned to normal.

The article also included statements from several of his friends. They said Jason went into Eden Hollow on a dare. That he was planning to spend the night out there alone. A camcorder was evidently out of his budget, and wouldn't work well in the dark anyway, so he brought a voice recorder instead.

It took me a whole weekend of scouring yard sales to locate a player. I listened to it in my kitchen with the black noise of the crickets bleeding in through the bug screens.

The tape began with what sounds like someone walking through underbrush. I could hear the regular dry scrape of fabric, like the recorder was swinging from a clip and brushing against Jason's backpack. Beneath and around that sound, leaves crackled and sticks crunched. Footfalls scuffed the earth. Then the first instance of Jason's voice.

Just snuck onto the property known as Eden Hollow. Been hearing legends about this place all my life. So now I've come here to confront and hopefully record whatever it is that gives these woods such a bad reputation. Wish me luck, friends; I only brought one pair of underwear.

The kid had a good, clear speaking voice, and the precocious confidence of a young man used to getting big parts in school productions. I found myself liking him immediately, which made listening to the rest of the tape difficult. More walking sounds, and then nothing, until...

Getting grody already folks. You ain't going to believe this.

Jason was out of breath and overloud. It's possible he was acting but if so, he had some talent.

After scouting around some I set up camp near the small crick at the base of the hollow. It wasn't easy to find good kindling; everything down here is damp and covered with fungus, but I managed to get a little fire going.

For a while everything seemed normal. Then I felt... well, it's pretty hard to describe actually. Like a really big muscle was contracting beneath me. Like... like it was my turn in the parachute at summer camp. When everyone else was yanking hard from the edges and it tightened underneath me.

It doesn't make any sense but I think that flexing did something to me. Messed with my balance or... I don't know. Gave me whaddayacallit... vertigo. I fell on my butt and when I got back to my feet, I felt sick. I mean really sick. I almost never throw up and next thing I know I'm on my knees ralphing like my stomach is fixing to crawl through my mouth. Like something is trying to turn me inside out.

Once I stopped puking I lay down on my back, but I couldn't shake the idea that I was bleeding out. Well, not bleeding, exactly. More like that little shiver you get when you take a piss. But worse. Oh my God, so much worse. Like something... important. Something... critical... I don't know... my spirit or something... like it was leaking out of me. I kept checking my clothes and the ground beneath me but everything was so damp I couldn't tell what was going on.

I'm staying put for now. I feel like shit and I want to be in my own bed so bad but I'm not sure I can get myself out of here in the dark. Not like this. I already got into the tent and now I'm lying here trying to distract myself by talking into this tape recorder. Soon as it's light out I'm getting the hell out of here.

The recording smash-cuts again, dropping out and picking up abruptly. The sudden edits make it impossible to tell how much time has passed.

So, um, I definitely just felt something big swim through the dirt beneath me and I'm going crazy in here wondering what the eff can do that.

[Indistinct noise]

There!

[Indistinct noise repeated]

Aw, man. Eff this!

[Zipper sound and rustle of nylon flap. A few steps…silence…then a few more steps.]

Oh my God.

And then he was running. Or falling. I heard grunts and meaty thumps. An intake of breath and then… violence. The kid screamed, loud, but the scream was cut off and strangled into a high-pitched squeal, then doubled, as if in mockery. More screams. For mercy. For his mom. A lot more screams. Some human but some—

I stopped the tape and pushed the player away. I thought of Jason's parents listening to what I'd just heard, after the recorder was found in the woods near his abandoned tent. I pictured the shock and joy in their faces when he turned up still alive. Then I imagined that joy slowly draining away into the black soil of what he had become.

***

The unorthodox size and high paper quality of the black and white photograph suggested amateur development, but its exact age was hard to guess. It appeared to depict the upper torso of a heavyset man writhing on the ground. I immediately thought of that word *writhing* because the face was in such poor focus, but it is possible the figure was motionless and the face was blurred by damage or some other distortion. I say *torso* because the arms and legs were missing. A shovel lay in the foreground, its head darkened with shadow or damp.

Written in the white border below: *Initial tests show abnormal mortality and an extremely elevated tolerance for pain.*

I ignored the floppy disk for a while, uncertain how to even go about determining what was on it. Then I remembered Mike Watts, an old high school classmate who ran the last computer repair shop in town. Or used to, anyway—as I learned when I drove by his vacant storefront. Good thing I still remembered where he lived.

"Go to hell," he said to my knock. "I don't take solicitors."

"It's Jimmy Ballard, Mike. I'm not here to sell anything."

"Whaddaya want then? Guys like you already put me out of business."

"That's pretty goddamn specious, Mike. I fix up and flip old houses; I don't own stock in Best Buy."

Long pause, then: "Whaddya want, Jimmy?"

"To pay you for your expertise."

That opened the door and got me inside. Mike looked bad, pale and unshaven. His house was in awful disarray. Every surface was still piled with gear. Some of it looked like unsold inventory of recent make, but the majority had enough dust and grimy beige plastic to suggest a tech hoarding problem.

"I drove by the store," I said. "When did you go out of business?"

"Sometime around Y2K. It just took a while for my ass to catch up."

"Got anything that can read this?" I held up the old floppy.

Mike's eyebrows arched. "What's on it?" he asked. "A copy of Zork?"

"I don't know. That's where you come in."

"Okay, then. What's so important about finding out?"

"Like I said, no idea. Maybe nothing."

"Is that all I'm going to get?"

"It concerns some land I bought. I'd rather not say any more."

"Okay, mystery man. I do in fact have a couple five-and-a-quarter-inch drives sitting around here somewhere, but no idea if they still work and nothing that's been turned on this century with the right cabling or add-on card. Leave the disk with me and I'll—"

"I'll wait," I interrupted. "And if it's all the same to you, I'd rather be the only one who sees what's on it."

"It's your dime. Speaking of which…"

"How does a hundred bucks sound?"

"Make it two hundred and I'll throw in a dial-up modem and a dot matrix printer."

"I have one hundred-dollar bill in my wallet. You can have it, or I can let the A/V club at the high school take a shot at it."

Mike shook his head and mumbled something about zoomers that I couldn't hear. He pointed to his easy chair and an array of remotes. "Give me an hour. There's a two-liter in the fridge."

It took him three hours, actually, because the disk was formatted for a Mac, not Microsoft, and his first setup failed to read it. Mike swore he still had a working Apple IIe boxed up somewhere, and he did, only it was under a metric crapload of CRT monitors, PC towers, and other crap in his garage. By some miracle it still booted. Mike stuck around long enough to show me how to execute the small Applesoft BASIC program saved to the disc under the filename 'EdenHollow'. Once run, the screen went blank save for the instruction to

PRESS ANY KEY

Each time I did, another row of characters added to the bottom of the screen. As the lines scrolled up, two heads emerged a short-ways apart, inscrutable ASCII faces drawn with Xs, Os, underscores and vertical bars. Then shoulders and torsos: more bars, dashes, slashes forward and back. They rose up like things growing from the negative space offscreen. The figures seemed child-like in proportion, and were identical to each other save that the interior of the figure on the left was filled with random combinations of the letters A, C, G, and T, and the figure on the right was empty and blank—just an outline. Once both reached full height, each additional key press directed a total migration of the letters. They spilled from a seam that opened in the left one's gut, dripping to the ground like alphabet soup before rising up again and filling the empty figure on the right.

When the process was complete, when the second was full of the As, Cs, Gs, and Ts, and the first was hollow, each subsequent key press sucked the left figure down into the nothingness offscreen. At the end of this low-res burial, the right figure smiled. Its mouth changed from the flat horizontal of four underscores to just two of them, centered between a pair of parentheses.

I saved the videotape for last. In terrible focus and poor lighting, it depicted the so-called eviction of a middle-aged woman who someone had chained to a tree. I couldn't be certain it was real. Hell, I couldn't watch more than a minute of it, but what I did see was convincing enough to send me over to Eden Hollow with a new stack of Private Property and No Trespassing signs and a much bigger lock for the gate.

***

This time I was actually relieved to find Routledge there waiting for me. I had so many questions for him. The man's posture was all wrong, though. At first I thought that he had chained himself to the gate and passed out like an activist trying to block the entrance to a nuclear power plant. The truth only came clear after I'd parked and walked close enough to see him slumped over, his neck yoked with his belt and his blue-black face yanked skyward. On his chest was a crude sign made of wood and twine. On the wood—

The smell of death punched me in the nose. I stumbled back and dry heaved. I tried to breathe through my mouth for a few minutes before I could straighten up and try again.

The sign read:

ENJOY YOUR EVICTION ☺
AUTOPSY REQUESTED!

***

Sheriff Ames asked me how long I had owned the property, and whether I was acquainted with the man the county medical examiner was zipping into a bag. I stuck to the basic facts of our previous encounter, and Ames filed Routledge's death as a suicide. Which it was, I think, only not for the reasons assumed.

Ames has decent instincts for a small-town cop. After some thought, he asked me if there wasn't something more I wanted to tell him. I didn't lie to him. I just shook my head a little. As Ames was leaving, I asked him whether the man's final wish would be granted.

He took off his sunglasses and gave me another hard look. "You know any good reasons for it?"

His question dangled like a badly tied lure with a clearly visible barb, and I left it there, spinning in the wind.

I'd arrived just after nine, on what was then a bright morning. By the time Ames and the medical examiner left, a strange conspiracy of sun and cloud was throwing a sickly yellow light over everything. A short debate flared between my ears. The winning argument went something like this: If I kept to the perimeter while posting my signs, and never actually went into the hollow, I shouldn't be affected. Not any more than I already was. I think this was what Routledge hoped to prove with his morbid request.

I kept my head on a swivel as I walked the property line, hanging signs every couple hundred yards or so. I did not see or experience anything I could put on a police report, but as I worked I did succumb to a strange and seductive idea.

Like the child whose own eyes insist the moon is following him, I came to believe that whatever inhabited Eden Hollow was tethered to me now. That it paced and welcomed my progress around its flank, and that wherever I went, whichever angle I might take to catch it unawares, it would always be watching me with its basilisk gaze, hoping I might come a little closer. That in seeing me, it was already teaching me new ways of seeing myself.

The feeling peaked as I neared the edges of the lowlands that give the place its name. The distance, the crowding trees, the fading light, and the steep cant of the landscape all prevented me from seeing very far into the ravine. But still I looked, long and hard, certain that now, at last, the revelation would come. The sun continued to sink and shadows grew long in the teeth, nibbling at the edges of things—until a certain stack of ovoid shapes emerged at the tree line, reminiscent of the roughly sketched human in the Polaroid. Again, it might have been nothing more than an illusion formed by the voids between actual life forms. It seemed amorphous and unconfined by the normal rules of spatial location. By just relaxing and refocusing my eyes I could make the thing recede into the background or pull forward into focus. I'm not sure if anything moved, but at one point it did appear to change. Something extended from its upper section—a limb, or some other appendage, or maybe just the suggestion of one. And then the limb was beckoning to me. And then I was waving back.

And then I was walking towards it at a terrific pace.

I dropped my arm and froze the second I realized what I was doing, but not before I was overcome by the certainty that I was now, if not always, both the sender and receiver of whatever message was being conveyed. That my inability to understand it rested solely with my refusal to listen more closely to myself.

That cleaving sensation only grew, it never diminished. Not when I finished posting my signs. Not when I retreated to the dash-lit cocoon of my pickup. And certainly not now, as I stand again at the edge of Eden Hollow and make peace with an overwhelming urge to close the distance.

I believe that phantom arm is something like a vestigial antenna. I believe the odd painful sensation I feel is not so much a longing for a missing limb, but a severed line of communication. An opportunity for improvement. I believe the signals I cannot yet decode are instructions for my evolution. Whatever I walk towards is what will make me whole. The meat and mind I leave behind are nothing I will need.

What is the difference after all, between your average human being and a clever simulacrum built with borrowed matter and sent into the world without the dimmest knowledge of its maker or barest understanding of its purpose? What is risked by shedding that rotting coil and seeking a new and better form? More importantly, what might be gained?

There is only one way to find out.
But don't take my word for it.
Come to Eden Hollow and see for yourself.
And when you do, friend, please enjoy your eviction. ☺

Brodkin's Demesne

Bethany screams again but nothing changes. Pete doesn't appear and the droning just goes on. If anything it seems to grow louder, and larger. As if feeding on her distress. At times like these, the sound attacks her from everywhere at once, drilling her eardrums and squeezing her skull with a psychosomatic contraction so strong it feels like her eyes might actually pop under the strain. Fifty yards of gradual downslope separate her from the old barn where Pete is working, but the way is so littered with rotting cicada exuviae that it might as well be the Salton Sea. She hasn't ventured into the backyard since the cicadas started molting, and she sure as hell isn't going to try now. Feeling trapped and infantile, she stamps her feet, balls her hands, and yells Pete's name into the throbbing void.

All she wants is for him to take a break and watch the sunset with her in the metal rockers she rescued from slow disintegration behind the garage. Desperate for an escape, she leveraged them into her trunk and drove them over an hour away to have a sandblaster scour away all the rust. Now, after two coats of primer and four coats of paint, they look good enough for a vintage décor magazine.

Her voice eventually cracks and gives out. Extracting her cell phone, she furiously texts him her request. How pathetic, that this has become the protocol for communicating with him while he is working, as outlined in a bulleted email the bastard had the temerity to title *My New and Unalienable Rights of Immaculate Domain.*

After a punitive delay, he finally pokes his head out of the barn, lumbers across the Salton Sea, and climbs the back steps like a man returning from a massacre. By then the light has changed and all the colors are fleeing. He stands there glowering at her from the shadowed edge of the porch, and for a moment he looks like he has been decapitated by the dark. The impression fades as he passes into the small square of light thrown from the window, and his face becomes a face again. He accepts the sweating HopDevil she offers and her pique flares when he just slumps into one of the resurrected chairs without so much as a *thank you ma'am.* She gives him sixty seconds to sulk and then lobs him a softball.

"Did you get a lot done today?"

"It's a big job," he says without looking at her.

The snarky part of her wants to ask which, the unfinished studio or the overdue film project? "But it's going well? You're feeling good about it?"

"I can't even see the edges of it yet."

She gives up and frowns at him while he stares into the gathering night, wondering how much longer she can ignore the signs of his breakdown. Even in good light he has become a crazed and sinister presence, nothing at all like the guy once voted Most Likely to DJ Your Wedding. His usually trim beard has grown wild and pubic. His kind brown eyes are now perpetually cut to a menacing squint. With all that sweat and dirt caked into his crow's feet, he looks less like an in-demand sound engineer and more like someone auditioning for the evil shaman part in the independent horror film he was supposed to be done scoring by now. Asked to sign a standard nondisclosure, he treats the project like some kind of national secret. She hasn't been permitted to *see* more than ten seconds of it, but she *hears* more than enough, thank you very much, and it's a damn good thing their nearest neighbors are so far away or else they'd both have to answer for all the demented noise leaking into the world through his studio monitors. After weeks of ransacking occult websites, poorly scanned grimoires and dodgy transcriptions of ancient incantations, all for the right concatenation of creepy syllables, he has recently begun to assemble and blare endless iterations of the results: chants and shrieks, dead tongue twisters, twenty ear-shredding tracks layered atop each other and digitally degraded into an unspeakable glossolalia. Nothing was *right*. Nothing was *massive* or *malevolent* enough for him.

He'd been threatening to build an infinite baffle subwoofer for years, and now he finally had the space and the perfect excuse. With a dozen eighteen-inch drivers, each as heavy as an anvil, and crude plans he found on the internet, he turned the old stone barn into a mammoth resonator. The first time he fired it up she was inside the house, and even at that distance every collective thrust of the voice coils felt like a medicine ball thrown at her chest by an irate gym teacher. One time she got caught outside near the barn when the bass dropped, and it hit her like a seizure: total body static. She actually peed herself a little. She had no idea how he could stand it at such close range.

When she asked him what he was trying to do, he made even less sense than usual. He was *trawling the abyss*, he said. *Making waves* and *taking soundings*. Seeing *what showed up in the backwash*. The infrasonics alone made her feel like putting a gun in her mouth. She complained about it every chance she got, but instead of dialing it back Pete devolved into a little kid given permission to play with a very big gun—trigger happy and surely going deaf. When the cicadas first emerged she actually thanked them for providing him a new distraction.

To a friend, or maybe her mother, she might admit that she was also unwell. That this desperate enforcement of a happy-hour drink was every bit as much for her sake as his. She hadn't believed her freelance friends when they warned her working from home wasn't as ideal as it sounded. Particularly this home. Pete's sound experiments were bad enough, but if she had known a few months after they moved in that a billion cicadas would boil up from the earth and foul her painstakingly decluttered headspace, she would have postponed this whole horse-country experiment, stayed on at the firm downtown, and banked another year of her old salary.

But then they would have missed their shot. An old Swarthmore friend who worked at a boutique estate agency and shared her taste for country chic had sent her some photos before it was officially on the market, and she'd known right away it was exactly what she wanted. Unlike all those badly stuccoed McMansions in West Chester, full of gypsum board and Chinese plywood, Brodkin's Demesne was built with local blue stone and old growth oak. And how cool was that name? In her wildest fantasies she'd never dreamed she'd live on a named estate. Who cares if nobody could pronounce it or tell her what it meant? And sure, the place was drafty and dark and the bathrooms were tiny with bad plumbing, and *things*, multiple *things*, were living in the attic, scampering across their bedroom ceiling all night and pissing wherever they damn well pleased—but it had original 19th-century wainscoting for Christ's sake, four separate chimneys, mantled fireplaces in almost every room, stained glass windows on the second-floor landing. It even had a small orchard. She didn't know a damned thing about maintaining fruit trees, but she could always learn, couldn't she?

On a purely conceptual level, she found it tragic that after so many generations of stewardship the surviving owners wanted no part of their ancestral estate beyond their cut of its sale. On a personal level, it was very fortunate indeed. Not only did the property boast one of the oldest, stateliest homes in the Brandywine Valley—the perfect demographic for her new private law practice—it also came with a stone barn of even hoarier vintage, where Pete could build his dream studio. Compared to a loft or a rowhome, it was a virtual fiefdom. And what little Philly latchkey girl wouldn't jump at the chance of owning her own magic kingdom?

If only it wasn't under attack by biblical plague. It didn't help that alarmist blogs were going all caps-lock, exclamation-point about it. Clickbait loonies calling it a rogue brood and claiming it was proof of climate meltdown. According to them, periodical cicadas were genetically programmed to return in only thirteen or seventeen-year cycles. Nobody could explain the prime number connection, but none of the known populations lined up with this surprise emergence.

Bethany takes another large swig of wine and reminds herself that even such extreme events had to follow biological rules. It's not like cicadas were immortal. Or even remotely dangerous, for that matter. To humans anyway. She only had to survive about four more weeks of their monotone sex song and then it'd be all wildflowers and honeysuckle. Assuming Pete came out of his funk and they were able to keep up with the payments.

Failure on that front was not an option. Throwing the full-count curveball had been her call, so if it didn't work out, she would be the one to catch all the blowback. And accepting blame wasn't exactly her forte. Pete had warned her leaving the city would change the trajectory of their relationship in unpredictable ways, but she needed to ground him somehow if she ever hoped to have a kid, and she wasn't sure how many innings they had left in them. So far, all they had produced were balks.

Sitting there, slugging wine and waiting for Pete to mumble an excuse and retreat back to the barn, she began obsessing over the dreaded D word again. How embarrassing it would be, and how devastating. Divorce, she could handle—but *defaulting*? Ye gods forbid. All they needed was a good pep talk, maybe a huddle with a life coach. Lord knew Pete had clocked long, strange hours managing the studio downtown. Back then neither of them ever got home before dark, but at least when they were together, they were *together*. Something atrophied when they began spending all their time at this one address. They forgot how to warm up, what the signals meant. After a couple rounds of perfunctory sex to break in the old place, Pete started holing up in his barn. Now he only came out for meals and materials. The renovation was taking way too long. She'd told him to hire somebody, but he was too damn stubborn.

One day, when the cicadas really started blaring, Pete stood down his sonic canon and came out to mike the orchard with the little portable rig he used for custom Foley effects. She watched him through the blinds in their bedroom, and got her first honest sounding of the bitterness building between them. Instead of alarm or empathy, she felt a strange jolt of pleasure when he flipped on the power and threw off the headphones like they had shocked him. She'd warned him they got loud enough to cause permanent hearing loss, but he didn't believe her. She went into another room to get some laundry done, and when she came back a half hour later he was still there, in the same spot. But the headphones were back on, and he was standing way up on his toes, his posture twisted and rigid, as if frozen in convulsion. It dawned on her that he might be having a stroke, and her detachment cracked. She rushed downstairs and ran out to him, ready to call an ambulance, and found him blinking at her like she was the crazy one.

"Can you hear it?" he asked.

"Of course I can hear it. What's wrong with you?"

"It's so beautiful."

"You're losing your shit, Pete. *Please* get it together."

"Just listen," he said, offering her the headphones. But she didn't want to listen. She just wanted it to end. And one day it did end. Just not in the way she expected.

***

She wakes to the sound of her skull shattering. An interval of raw panic before the mandibles crushing her face retract into her subconscious, and she realizes that what she really heard was the implosion of the wine glass she had fallen asleep still clutching, and that blood—her blood—is pouring from her palm like a stigmatic in a giallo film. She leaps to her feet so fast the head rush nearly knocks her out. She reels, reaches out for balance, plants a red handprint on the upholstery, and narrowly avoids knocking over all the empty bottles lined up on the floor. Even so, the damage is done; her new white couch is a crime scene.

The cut is deep and nasty. She flushes it at the sink until her hand goes numb and the bleeding slows enough to hunt for shards. Another near faint while pulling wide the gash. The cold water helps deaden the pain, but a strange inability to focus properly makes her wonder whether she somehow cracked her skull after all. Recollection coagulates around the wound.

This time Pete never came in from the barn. Never responded to her text. Tired of waiting, tired of being ignored, she went back inside and opened one of the really good bottles of wine she'd been saving to celebrate completion of the studio. This much she can remember—but was that last night, or the night before? Her mind aches, and little mystery why. All the available evidence suggests an extended and quite abnormal binge. She doesn't notice what has happened until she cuts off the water, bandages her wound and steps through the screen door into a stark and sepulchral hush.

Sometime during the night the cicadas went silent. Nary a tymbal is vibrating.

Relief crumples her into a dropped-puppet slump until another stab of pain pulls her strings taut again. The pain makes her alert, and angry. Where the hell is Pete? She could have bled to death for Christ's sake. She holds the wounded hand by the wrist, as if taking her own pulse. Down the steps like this, pale and pissed, she wades into the Salton Sea, into the minefield of ick. Legions of discarded skins crunch underfoot and their stench of briny rot fouls her airways like a summer dumpster behind a seafood joint. The smell is somehow exaggerated by the silence. In the wake of the eternal drone, this preternatural hush is unnerving and surreal, so much so she cannot quite convince herself she isn't dreaming it. They are deathly quiet, but they haven't left, she realizes, as she begins to spy them by the thousands, roosting in the shrubbery. Like a trenched army waiting for the order to attack.

Freaked out by the thought of all those red eyes upon her, she hurries now into a jittery stutter step. Fighting one-handed to open the barn door, she stumbles in through the dust. The smell is even stronger inside. Long white tarps hanging from the two-story rafters seal off the gear room from the active renovation and give the gloomy vestibule the kinetic emptiness of a recently evacuated theater. Too spooked to linger, she pushes through an overlapping seam and into the makeshift studio.

The room appears empty save Pete's main console and abutting banks of vintage gear. All the knobs and dials and buttons vaguely remind her of the multitude waiting silently outside, an interlinked network of resurrected things, exhumed and assembled for some obscure purpose. She approaches his empty chair and lowers herself into it. A fractal screensaver gyrates in microcosmic infinity until she nudges the mouse and unveils the stack of spectral insanity hiding behind it. Jagged lines vault and plummet across the screen to pitches far beyond the range of human hearing. Below them is an arrowed play icon too tempting to ignore. Clicking it instantly drives her backwards and out of the chair. She crouches and covers her ears, assaulted by a torrent of noise not even the damned should endure. The whole barn shakes with it; a hurricane of oscillating frequencies given visible agency by the motes of dust vibrating in the light-spoked air like primitive organisms striving to evolve. She can't move, can't think, can hardly breathe until the recording plays itself out some scrambled length of time later.

She lies back and takes her hands away from her ears. Only from this prone perspective is she able to locate what appears to be the remains of Pete.

Her first thought is violent electrocution. What else could explain the big brittle carapace stuck so far up the load-bearing post? She gets to her feet, circling around to see, and freezes when her new vantage reveals a tenuousness and a transparency not evident from the rear. This withered amber husk cannot be her husband. That torn paper mask must not be his face. As if in confirmation, a scuttling sound beyond the curtain swivels her head.

"Pete?"

Shock drops a veil of protective detachment over her senses, slowing her galloping panic into a bridled curiosity. She follows the sound back through the winding-sheet partition, back through the vestibule, and into the ancient heart of the barn.

The smell is strongest there. Loamy rot and acid bile. The smell of evisceration. Sections of the hand-hewn floorboards have been torn away and a wide burrow gapes below. She grabs a work light hanging from a nail, and as she leans down to look, the newborn brood king contracts its dorsal thorax and unfurls its massive, vein-mazed wings across the rafters over her head. In its teneral state it is white as a grub save for its bulbous, blood red eyes. It glistens like an avenging angel when she spins and shines the light upon it. Lancing halfway to the floor, its barbed aedeagus twitches in expectation. The old beam bends and groans back into shape when the brood king lifts from its perch and falls like lightning, pinning her to the earth. For a spell of time both eternal and brief, the heavy silence is punctured by the screams and prayers of unnatural selection.

***

In a dark corner of the loft with a clear view of what just happened. Pete crouches and shakes. Blood paints his jowls in symmetrical trails and drips onto his portable rig. He'd been monitoring the pupa in secret for days, acclimating to the reality of it and listening for signs of its emergence. But it was only this morning, when it wriggled from its shell and blew out his eardrums with its first, titanic sounding, that he finally understood his role in all this.

He was born and brought here to be the brood king's recordist—its scribe and herald. Whatever revelations were encoded in its apocalyptic trumpet must be documented and disseminated. And so he kept recording, despite the fact that he himself could not hear it anymore—a blessing for certain while it ravaged the poor soul who was once his wife and thrust her still-living body into the waiting burrow. Presumably to feed and shelter its successor even as it grew within her. Whatever the case, some things are better left unheard.

He climbs down when the brood king flies through the barn doors Bethany left open for it. In his simple anthropomorphic projection, he suspects that it will be hungry or sleepy afterward. He hopes this distraction will give him enough time to get to the house and grab some more tape before anything else important happens.

He is half-right, at least. After centuries of chthonic stasis, the great beast is anything but tired. But it is ravenous, and prowling the airspace above its demesne for a favorite snack. Pete's fatal error, beyond awakening it in the first place, is a failure to guess what that might be. It drops from the sky the second he emerges. Needless to say, he never hears it coming.

***

One of the many wonders of magicicada physiology is their ability to cork food sources with viscous saliva once they are done feeding, thereby preserving the leftovers. Pete has no time to ponder the ramifications or evolutionary genius of this before a six-foot stylet spears him through one eye socket and deftly lobotomizes him while siphoning a measure of his cerebrospinal fluid. Over millennia of trial and error, the brood kings have learned that all large mammals continuously produce this clear and nutrient-rich fluid. More, in fact, than they can ever use, so long as they are provided a minimal amount of sustenance, and the intrusions don't go too deep into their brains.

So in a very real way, both Bethany and Pete got what they wanted. She was given a child, of sorts, and he a purpose that, properly managed, just might last him the rest of his days. And though Pete now lacks any ability to communicate his thoughts on this arrangement, the permanent wink and asymmetrical smirk it affixes on his face records at least some manner of awestruck appreciation.

Unmoved by this temporal drama, the imago horde end their intermission and begin to sing anew. For like all things born in the image and beneath the watchful gaze of their god, they too are

135

hardwired to honor an ancient ritual they cannot understand. To persist in the glorious hope of being born again.

RED BLOOM, WHITE VAN, BLUE VELVET

You cut school the day the Challenger exploded, so you didn't see it live like all the other kids. You heard about it that night, of course, and when you did you felt a sick black horror, imagining those astronauts in freefall and with plenty of time to scream before they suffocated and smashed apart on impact.

Skipping wasn't your usual M.O.—you liked school. Especially science, and those shop classes they don't teach anymore. You spent that day freezing your fingers stiff around the handle of an old rusted shovel because you'd woken up to a heat-less house, and instead of siphoning oil from your neighbor's tank like any common hoodlum would, or asking Larry for an advance, you decided that was the day to search The Dismal for the trashbag of cash you'd heard some local thief had stashed there before getting nicked by the cops.

A wicked cold snap sapped your heating oil supply. Your mother was still sleeping off a late shift when you shook her awake, your icepick finger on her pale exposed arm shocking her out of bed and into her ratty old robe. You thought it important to let her know you could see your breath. *Just put on a sweater,* she said, and shuffled to the bathroom. She couldn't afford to turn the thermostat any higher and risk running out entirely before she had any funds for the refill.

Right away you thought of The Dismal, that weird body of water hidden in the woods behind your house. If water had bodies, then this one was dead. *Water* and *woods* paint a pretty picture, but this place felt killed and discarded. It wasn't a lake. Hardly even a pond. Just a festering swamp of runoff at the bottom of a ravine between your house and what passed for the town center. In the absence of anything official, local kids coined all sorts of names for it: The Stinkhole, Lake Doom, The Black Lagoon. Your favorite was The Dismal. Nothing great about it and straight to the truth of its nature.

The Dismal froze during the coldest stretches, but otherwise it stayed wet and dark and dank enough to latch a kind of leech onto the local id. All sorts of dreadful stories were sucked up from its murk, enough to send someone like you searching, and a few were even true. The Dismal was in fact where some grade school kids found a girl named Sarah Monahan stuffed into the belly of a dead oak, strangled with shoelaces her killer had left tied into a perfect little bow.

Almost a decade earlier, The Dismal was also where they apprehended a local man by the name of Ronnie Walsh. Ronnie's mother needed some kind of spine corrective surgery they couldn't afford, and so he set out to steal the funds. He hit two small banks and a convenience store for good measure but whether he *actually* buried his loot before they caught him, well, that was anybody's guess. You sure as shit didn't find it in any of the three dozen holes you dug that day.

The other stories were more slippery and outlandish—as if to push aside those sad, hard truths with more entertaining fare. But even so, such folklore seldom fails to instruct. Back then you had a fancy theory about urban legends, influenced by your love of science and astronomy. You thought of tall tales as packets of radiation emanating from real events. Like the red shift in stars, a distortion that encodes certain truths about distance, velocity, wavelength. Deviations from the norm that reveal its actual position. Aftershocks not yet suffered, but empirically foretold.

It took NASA until late April to find and collect the astronauts' remains. You remember the story in the paper, just a few days before the news about Chernobyl broke. You remember thinking it wasn't just more bad news that had broken, but everything else along with it.

You didn't believe in things like ghosts, or witches, or demons. You took your science too seriously. But in that science, especially at its edges, you sensed an infinite expanse populated by things far worse. You were tracked level two or three for everything else but honors and AP for science, and if AP Physics taught you anything about the real world, it was that everything is energy and energy always breaks down. And in that breaking down, it sends out invitations to observe its entropic collapse. One just has to know how to accept the invitation. You might never understand the math, but you knew damn well that dark matter had the greatest mass, the strongest pull.

Less of a mystery is the why. Your father left before your sense of self had fully formed. Lacking much else of note to shape a personality, his leaving became the last and most lasting step of that hardening. In the same way an infant's skull can flatten or otherwise squish out of shape before the fusing of the plates, up to a certain point your personality felt malleable and open. You weren't this or that, melancholic or bubbly, sloppy or neat, lazy or hyper, but somewhere in the middle. Your cracks formed in that firing. Nothing charming or distinctive, though. Nothing *wabi-sabi*. You've been morbid and brooding and distrustful ever since, but after the red bloom hit, those traits began to feel less like flaws and more like a latency; the nebulous signs of something larger collapsing in on itself, preparing to go nova.

Not long after Chernobyl, you came upon The Dismal and found it filled with blood. You knew it wasn't Sarah Monahan's. You knew it wasn't Pennywise come to clown around, however deep the dent

IT left on your mental nightstand. The fact that no one else was talking about the bloody water yet suggested not that you were hallucinating, but only that you were the first to see it. The blood was both an invitation and an augury.

Even later, after you learned it wasn't blood, that it was caused by toxic algae, you found the term *red bloom* so darkly apropos. By that point you had spun the worldview display case and chosen not rose but blood-tinted glasses. Donning them felt like staring into the sun with your eyes closed. Crimson-laced lids fluttering like flower petals against the constant urge to open wide and flood your soul with all that blinding pain. All that suffering. All those capillary connections, tapering to extremity. What if *you* were *IT* and there was no one else to tag? Red flags and red balloons. A red tide at ebb too soon to flow.

You couldn't afford a shrink. You couldn't even afford to dawdle. You were fifteen years old and running late for work.

***

WHITE VAN
"Think you could close up again tonight?"

You hear the words but your brain does nothing with them. You're too busy peering through one of the big plate windows that frame the front of Zoetrope Video. A few minutes earlier a white van pulled into the lot, but whoever was driving it has yet to come inside.

The driver lights a cigarette, and through the passenger window of the van you can briefly make out not just his head and shoulders but also someone smaller in the seat next to him. Their heads lean close, as if in conversation, and then closer. You relax a little and refocus. In your limited understanding, psychopaths don't kiss their victims, or take them to the video store. The darkness outside makes dim mirrors of the windows, so you can see yourself better than you can see the van. A growth spurt has stretched your once-soft torso like one of those Laffy Taffys you used to love, a weapons-grade candy that took a long time to eat and even longer to digest. For all you know a backlog still lingers in your intestines like Jabba's victims of the sarlacc.

The dirty reflection darkens your edges and drains your face of life. The way the counter bisects you at the waist completes the caricature. You are the fey fraternal twin of the Black Dahlia, whose halved corpse you first saw in a scrapbook of crime scene photos your buddy Ian lifted from Jimmy Mullin's pawn shop. At that point it was the saddest, grossest thing you'd ever seen. And yet also something like a glimpse of the world's true face. You stare into your dim reflection and use your fingers to stretch your mouth into a Glasgow smile.

"You going deaf?"

You flinch as if shoved. Larry is suddenly behind you, speaking into your ear.

"No problem," you say. "I got it."

"You sure?"

He's sensing some unease in your voice, but he probably thinks it's about closing the store on your own. You will have trouble getting your till to zero out, like always, but you're pretty sure you can handle re-shelving the returns, running the vacuum, and shutting down the DOS-based rental system. After that, all that's left is to turn out the lights and lock up. You've done it two or three times already and it makes you feel kinda badass. Or at least like less of a fuckup.

You nod and say, "I'm sure. Hot date?"

"Kind of. I'm DMing a new campaign tonight and I need to prep a little before my crew arrives."

Larry is thirty-something and already balding on top. He counters it by growing out his coils of kinky hair elsewhere. Like Weird Al riffing on a Gregorian monk. Beyond managing the store, he also runs a local chess competition over the summers and builds giant speakers in his garage. Larry's favorite bands are Rush and Yes. His definition of a great party always includes two mages and a Halfling thief. You know how uncool he presents to the world at large, but Larry's modest aspirations and dorky enthusiasms make you feel a lot better about your own. Last Monday night, the only day the store isn't open, he took you to see *Highlander* and you greeted each other the next day with a spontaneous bout of pretend swordplay while screaming, in shitty Scottish, *There can be only one!*

Even if you had nothing in common, you'd always appreciate Larry for breaking the rules and hiring you at fourteen, after you explained a bit about your situation. How much you and your mom needed the money. Now he even trusts you with a store key. Which is why you don't mention the van. You don't want to sound like a scared little kid.

Larry exits with an ominous *thunk.* The heavy, self-closing door in the back leads directly to where he parked, so he never even sees the white van. Not that it would have given him much pause. The store sits in a little cutout where the woods peter out and the town center begins. Older, cooler kids use the thin screen of trees behind the store as cover for parties and sex. Larry doesn't call the cops or tow anyone unless the lot is full or things get out of hand.

You don't realize how much you want a kegger to be the reason why the van is there until Larry pulls away in his Pontiac and the van's passenger, as if waiting for just this cue, gets outs of the van and starts walking toward the store. You look at your Casio Databank watch and see that it is five minutes before closing time.

The passenger is carrying a cardboard box and struggling a bit under its weight. What you can make out behind the box looks like an adolescent boy, thin and wiry like you, but younger and smaller. His slightness does nothing to ease your mind. Bad vibes are coming off this kid like solar flares. Your brain does another of its black magic tricks and conjures a dead bunny in the box. You're about to dash for the door and lock it when you realize you won't make it in time.

"Evening!" the kid says after bumbling backwards through the door. He carries the box to the counter, plops it down, and bares a big, sloppy smile. His chin barely clears the counter. A ball cap sits low and a bit askew on his head, blocking some of his face, but with a smile that wide it's hard to miss the fact that he sports a full set of dentures. You wonder why he looks so familiar, and then it

comes to you. He's like a mini version of the evil preacher in
Poltergeist II. You are no champion brusher, but you're having
trouble fathoming the type of neglect required to lose all your
teeth by twelve or thirteen. Must be a genetic thing, you think. Or
a disease. Unless they were knocked out....

"I'm sorry, but we're about to close."

"That's okay," he says, far too jovial for the occasion. "We're
hoping this won't take long."

"Are you a member here?"

"No."

"Is your father?"

"Is my what?"

You lift your chin towards the van, but he's already shaking his
head.

"That's not my father." The hat's too big and it slips around
enough to see that he is hairless. "Not in the way you mean."

His generic gray sweatshirt looks decades old and three sizes
too big. There's a smell coming off him that reminds you of the
dead possum you once buried under some leaves to save the skull.

"We're not from around here," he says, as if that explains it.

You know something really wrong is going on here, and part of
you feels for this strange kid, whatever his deal is, but he's making
you anxious as hell and you need him gone. You try to let him
down easy.

"Well, you need a membership card to rent and I've already
turned off the laminating machine."

"That's okay!" he repeats, all smiles again. Like he's one of
those animatronic mascots over at Circus Town Pizza and *Okay!* is
his catch phrase. The one his partner out there in the van would
probably rhyme with 'slay'. Or 'flay'. Or maybe 'obey'. "We're not
here to rent."

"You know this a video store, right?"

"We do, yes! We figured you'd know your way around a VCR."

You can't decide what is freaking you out more, his weird
antique adult way of speaking or his constant use of *We.* As if he
contains multitudes.

He opens the box flaps. To your relief there's no dead animal inside, just the VCR.

"Um, we don't really do repairs."

"Just do your best!"

"Well, okay, but my boss is the tech guy. If you leave it here, I can ask him to have a look at it tomorrow."

"We'd prefer that *you* give it a try."

"Well, I'm about to close. Either way, nobody can fix it tonight."

"*Please* don't say *that*!"

This is the first time he really sounds his age. As he says this, another red flare in the van outlines the large, dark figure behind the wheel. The flare grows and recedes like a slow breath, sucking the driver back into darkness.

The kid places his hands on the countertop, as if he might collapse without the support. The threat in his *please* is scary, but not nearly as scary as the curving black wires that poke from the tender webbing between his knuckles and snake up into his dirty sleeves. It could be some strange sort of costume. Or a medical device. It does remind you of the kind of apparatus used to pin a set of badly broken bones. You do your best not to stare, but your best isn't good enough. He drops his arms out of sight.

"Are you in some kind of trouble? Do you want me to call the cops?"

The kid shakes his head again, slow and serious. His skin is loose and wattled. His glassy eyes look like they might spin out of their sockets like errant skee balls. He snaps back into cheery mode. "*Please* don't! We just need your help with this VCR!"

You're beginning to think the quickest way out of this is to do what he asks. "What's the problem?"

"A tape is stuck inside. The tape means a lot to us. We're hoping you can get it out without damaging it." A pause to be sure you are looking at him. "But you can't watch it! It would be too intense for you."

You have no idea how he expects you to watch it without connecting it to a TV, but what he describes is actually something that falls within your skillset. Larry once showed you how, when the store machine did the same thing. There's a way to ease the tape off the drum assembly, but you'll have to open it up.

You duck your head and begin to root around in one of the drawers where you might find a screwdriver. You see a TV Guide and a menu from Carmine's Hoagies & Cold Cuts. You are about to slide over to the next drawer when you sense the kid is standing beside you.

On the other side of the counter.

The speed and silence with which he moved was almost impossible.

"What are you doing?" you say in a squeaking voice.

"Watching what *you're* doing." Eyes wide and swimming in their sockets.

"I'm looking for a screwdriver. Can you go back around, please? Only staff is allowed back here." At this range there's no mistaking that something is seriously off about this kid. His joints are fiddly, and his jaw hangs wrong.

"Do you have a button back here to alert the authorities?"

"Do I have a what? No."

"Weapons?"

You do a mental inventory. The screwdriver you seek might actually be your best bet. Beyond that, you have pens and pencils. A few spare rolls of change in your cash drawer. Only helpful if knew how to throw a real punch without breaking your hand.

You have scissors, but they are grade school surplus, not the sharp metal stabbers. You have a first edition paperback of *The Film Encyclopedia*. You have an auto rewind machine built like a red sports car, heavy enough to bludgeon someone to death, but only with inordinate enthusiasm.

You finally find the Philips head and screw up some courage. "I won't help you if you don't go back around."

The kid does as asked, but slowly, keeping his eyes on you the whole time.

"So what's so important about this tape?" You're not sure you want to know, but you have to do something to fill the dead air while you work on the VCR.

"It's rare," the kid says.

"What's on it?"

"Nothing you would like."

"How would you know?" you say, defensive. "I'm into some pretty edgy stuff."

"Oh yeah?" Leaning in. "Like what?"

"I've seen *Cannibal Holocaust* and *Cannibal Ferox*... both *Faces of Death*."

"Movies?" The kid leans back, unimpressed.

By now you've removed all the screws holding on the thin metal cover. You put some pressure on the retaining clips and turn it right side up to remove the lid.

"Nothing like that," the kid says. "It's more like a mirror."

You look up to find him staring down, seemingly entranced by the VCR's mechanics. You watch as he absently rolls his tongue across his upper dentures. To better secure them perhaps, or scrounge the remains of a snack.

"A mirror?" you ask, and stop to wait for his answer.

"Yeah. It's different for everyone."

You look back down and you see that the machine malfunctioned during playback. They were smart not to force it. A section of the tape is stretched across the rollers, hugging tight against the head. Any attempts to tug it out as-is would almost certainly tear the tape.

The cassette is generic and blank. It doesn't even have a stick-on label on its face. Perhaps the box holds the label. Perhaps the label would be incriminating.

Below the counter, within your reach, is a head cleaning tape that looks almost exactly like it. Used so long and often the labels have completely peeled away. Once you have extracted the stuck tape, with a little sleight of hand, you could swap out the tapes and see for yourself what all this fuss is about.

"Easy now," the kid says, as if he can hear your thoughts.

Your hands have already begun the rescue operation. You trace the linkage with your eyes, searching for the capstan motor that retracts the roller guides. When you find it, you rotate it until the guides are fully disengaged and the tape is no longer wrapped around the video head drum. At this point you must be especially careful not to snag the tape on anything on the way out, or let the cassette door snap closed and bite down on the still-exposed Mylar. You manually roll the loading motor with a gentle tug on its belt. You hold the cassette door open as it slowly lifts up toward the mouth of the machine.

You release a breath you didn't know you were holding.

You cannot fully extract the tape until the cassette door is closed, so you do your best to keep the exposed loop of tape tucked into the gap between the rollers. At the last moment, just before it comes free, the door snaps closed and the tape squirts through the slot like a can from an overeager soda machine. In your hurry to catch it, you fumble the tape and drop it onto the carpet of the elevated platform you are standing on.

The kid hisses. You crouch and pop back up with the head cleaner before he can prop his horrorshow hands onto the counter and look down at the real tape still sitting at your feet, brown loop protruding like a tongue.

"No harm done," you say. A big drop of sweat slides out of one armpit and traces a shivery slalom down your ribcage. You hold out the tape to show him. He snatches it and looks it over.

"You're lucky," the kid says.

You wonder if he's right. You wonder why on earth you did what you just did. You wonder what will happen when they figure it out. But most of all you wonder what prize you've won. You wonder what's on the tape.

"What do we owe you?" the kid says, surprising you.

"Nothing. It's on the house."

You've always wanted to say that, but when you do it dances through your head with a different meaning. Which house, exactly, and what pox have you put on it?

"Ah, but we insist," the kid says. "Everything has a price."

The kid leans over, disappearing from view. You wonder if he is pulling a similar kind of trick. Reaching down for one kind of payment and coming up with another.

He pops back into view clutching a tightly folded bill. Like he pulled it from his sock. When he hands it over it feels wet and slick, as if greased with sweat. You unfold it and find a hundred. The only ones you've seen before have been offered there in the store, all of them refused for lack of adequate change.

"I can't take that."

"Sure you can. Think of it like a bonus. You know, for overtime."

You are about to go on with your refusal when the kid places the VCR and the tape back in the box.

"Thanks! See you around," he says, and walks out.

Moments later the van pulls out of its space and coasts through the parking lot. The driver's side window is facing you as it exits, but the driver is just a dark shape abstracted by two layers of dirty windows. You keep looking and make out most of the license plate at least. If that's any indication of where they live, they will be several states away before they realize what you've done.

***

Your first instinct is to toss the tape into The Dismal on your way home. It is evidence, after all, both of your theft, and of whatever is on the tape. Instead you shove it into the farthest corner of your highest closet shelf. If you can forget about the tape, maybe you can forget about the kid and the faceless man in the van.

You know brains don't work that way. Especially yours. You hide out in your house eating giant bags of chips and two-liter sodas to fill the chasm of anxiety that you have opened inside yourself. When you leave your house, you walk with eyes scanning manically for a tail. You don't tell Larry about the weird kid. You don't tell anyone. Not even your mother, whose double shifts and silent sadness leave her far too brittle to bother. She's become like one of those rumors with only some basis in fact.

You hold out a little less than a week. You wait until your mother is working another double. You watch it on your attic bedroom rig, a VHS video camera you found in your neighbor's trash. The camera no longer records or charges a battery, but when plugged in it plays back just fine. You run its composite video out through an RF modulator and then connect that via coaxial to a 12-inch Quasar TV that wouldn't net ten bucks at a flea market. The rat's nest of cables looks ridiculous, and the signal is segmented by a rolling line of ground loop interference, but at least this way you can watch your cult favorites in peace, safe in cozy solitude, and drifting off to sleep is always an option. Except when it absolutely isn't.

You retrieve the tape from your closet, push in the cassette door release, check the slack, and tighten up the tape with your other thumb inside the right plastic gear. You insert, rewind, and hit play, remaining nearby in case you need to suddenly stop the screening. You want a good look, and you have no remote.

The suspense is extended by nearly four minutes of snowy black. You think the delay is probably intentional, so any unwanted watcher would assume it was blank and bail out before the feature began. Or maybe this was what the kid meant by a mirror. A Rorschach of static? But no, you just have to wait long enough.

What follows is hard to describe. Certainly not what you expected. No blood and no obvious torture. Less of a murder and more of a birth. But it scares you more than anything you will ever see for the rest of your life.

The footage opens in what looks like a basement workshop, starkly lit. The vast majority of the picture is filled with a metal table that glows a ghastly white. On the table is an intricate black wire frame, shaped like a small human. The sort someone might drape with strips of papier-mâché to make an effigy, or a Halloween decoration. A man steps in and out of the frame, retrieving and applying a strange material that looks like moldable flesh.

The shot is tightly cropped, roughly level with the table, so you cannot see anything of the figure above the sternum or below the upper thigh. The figure has a paunch. A hairy stomach bulges against his plain white undershirt. Wide hips in old jeans, held up with a belt. The belt buckle is stamped with a winged black beetle surrounded by glyphs in ornate filigree.

The sculpting footage goes on for over an hour, with lots of edits, so it is impossible to know how much time has actually passed. There is a certain tenderness to the way the flesh is applied and molded. Towards the end the eyes are installed. And then what looks to be the heart, only as Giacometti might sculpt it: black, pitted, undersized. The chest cavity is filled and smoothed over like a grave.

After completion the effigy is dressed: white cotton briefs, then a black t-shirt. There's something written on the shirt in bold blocky letters that you can't quite make out. Something about a better tomorrow. Sweat socks with double yellow bands around the top. Jeans. Ratty Chuck Taylors.

When he is done, the sculptor leans over and appears to give his creation mouth to mouth. He steps away from his work, allowing the camera to see it more clearly. What happens next is insane and impossible. When it gets off the table, there is a sound like a thousand finger joints popping at once. When it turns to face you, it wears a look of murderous recognition.

⁂

BLUE VELVET

You are just beginning to emerge from a fog of fear that obscured all but the most proximate aspects of your life. The next meal, the next class, the next shift at work. The fear has given you a different smell. Oily and animal. Your mother has complained about it.

It won't make much sense why, but you are only able to distract yourself from the fear and look a little further into the future thanks to a new film that is generating a lot of buzz. Larry wasn't a fan of *The Elephant Man* and he absolutely loathed *Eraserhead*, that "art-school abomination" you found so hypnotic and enthralling. So he's a strong pass on catching David Lynch's latest.

But you can't wait. You need to get your mind on something, anything else, and this flick sounds like just the ticket. Word is *Blue Velvet* is so weird and disturbing that the producers had to form their own distribution company to get it into theaters at all.

Premieres in New York and L.A. had lines around the block. Rumor has it the film is so intense it made one guy's pacemaker go haywire and nearly killed him. Never mind how much sense that makes.

You are used to seeing movies by yourself. It is already the minor addiction you will carry into adulthood. This is your seventh or eighth time already, and as much as you also enjoy going with others, these solo viewings always carry a little extra kick. You haven't done acid yet. Not even shrooms. But you understand the idea of a trip, at least intellectually, and this is your closest experience to date. With certain, prissier company you would change the metaphor and compare it to a kind of repeatable initiation. The anticipation. The rituals marking the beginning and the end. The tithing to the glass-boxed oracle. The ticketed permission to pass through the doorway and across the threshold between real and make believe. The tunnel in, the dropping into darkness, the blinding re-emergence. That strange sense of being both utterly alone and completely connected, through some magical medium, to a company of fellow initiates. The out of body states, the stages of suspended disbelief.

Even when the movie sucks, it always takes you somewhere. In this case you walk, and not just to town, but fifteen fucking miles. Out of town and across the river to an arthouse theater and the closest place where *Blue Velvet* is playing. You still don't have a license, no car to drive if you did, and no one else to drive you. Your bike is busted and buses don't run that way—but anyway, the walking will help you clear your head.

Or it would, if only you weren't being followed.

You have no idea how long the white van was pacing you. It's mid-October and you are halfway across the bridge. The wind is coming off the river in a cruel, unbroken blast. Head down, hands in pockets, Walkman blaring *Bela Lugosi's Dead* by Bauhaus, your sense of the world around you is even further deadened by a thick black hoodie pulled far enough to obscure your face. Your eyes are slits that crop your whole world down to a snorkel-mask oval. Your outsized feet in battered black Chucks slap the cement in involuntary allegiance to the scratchy beat. You feel electric and impervious, a walking third rail.

Until you clock the white van. It's moving at a crawl when you see it, as if waiting for you to notice it is there. When you lift your head and snatch back your hood it speeds up a bit and passes. You check the plate but it isn't the same, and you can't decide whether that means anything definitive. Can't you get a new one at the DMV? You watch it gradually recede around a soft bend across the bridge and then dip down onto Main Street. You kill the tunes and never pull on your hood or drop your head again the whole rest of the way to the theater.

Blue Velvet may be hot in New York and L.A., but it ain't killing it in bumfuck, PA. You're right on time but no line waits and very few cars are parked in the lot. You know the kid working the booth, so no trouble getting in, but you can't concentrate on the small talk he tries to make, some fanboy rumor about Lynch showing up unannounced at certain screenings. You're still too freaked about the van, so you beg off and head in. You grab a popcorn and a cherry Coke from the concession stand. You're the first one in and have your pick of seats. You sit dead center four rows back. The house lights are already down.

Something about coming in from the cold always makes you feel on the edge of a faint. The white screen against the black darkness only makes it worse. Pushbar shutter clicks throw doorways of light onto the screen as a few others slip into the theater, but they all sit behind you and several rows away. Nerves or a hesitance to puncture the silence keep conversation hushed and infrequent. You flash back to what the kid in the booth was repeating, that rumor about David Lynch liking to sneak into poorly attended screenings, to peep the Everyman faces of his audience. You have no idea if any of this is true. Lynch has never admitted to it. But didn't he go to art school over in Philly?

All of this extra build-up means that when the movie starts you are prepared to experience it as something more than a movie. Those opening credits against the undulating folds of the blue velvet curtains trap your eyes in an electric-blue kelp forest and prime you for the relentless waves of color cues to come. The red roses, the red fire engine, the red stop sign, the red dress, the red lamp shade, the red car in the driveway…

The red tide is aflood. The red bloom has bled all the way out of your brain and into the projection booth. The Norman-Rockwell-on-acid tableau of the suburban homeowner's stroke, while watering the lawn, on such a nice day. The only witness is a baby sticking a red popsicle into its red mouth as it totters towards this spastic effigy of capricious suffering. Otherwise he's alone, writhing on his back in a mud puddle of his own making as his rabid lapdog snaps at the unleashed spray of his unattended garden house. And if all that didn't draw you out of your physical body and into Lynch's latest fugue, he drags you down, down, down to the ground through a tunnel in the scything grass blades and dumps you like an undertaker into the alien insanity of an insect chorus.

Blue Velvet has barely begun.

Five minutes in, right about the time Jeffrey Beaumont finds the severed ear in the field, your already rocketing anxiety hits escape velocity when someone takes the seat directly behind you. You swivel your head just enough to confirm their presence, but dare not turn completely around.

The driver of the white van is either sitting behind you or he is not. The act of looking will be what makes it so. You must look, and yet you must not. This Schrödinger's cat mind trap works on you like a masonry chisel, calving off a self-protective remnant of you, so that you experience the rest of that strange and terrible film in a state of disassociated parallax. You watch *Blue Velvet* not only as the traumatized boy sitting in the fourth row, not only as the faceless psychopath sitting in the fifth, but also as another, far older and far colder you sitting in the sixth behind him.

This older, colder you is a golem with only one job. If the faceless man in the fifth row moves even the slightest bit to harm you, this sixth-row you will lean forward and cinch a homemade garrote around his neck. If D&D has taught you nothing else, it has taught you this. The deadliness of any given fantasy weapon depends entirely on its particulars. This garrote is made from a fifteen-inch length of guitar string wrapped around two lag bolts and pinned to their centers between washers and opposing nuts. It fits nicely in the hands and makes quicker work of a usually slow murder method. The man from the white van will be dead before he can speak, before anyone in the theater even realizes what is going on. Your sixth-row bodyguard will call for help, mumble something about the man choking on popcorn, and slip out in the confusion.

This ridiculous fantasy allows you to stay put and focus your fourth-row self on the film. To fully grok its subtext. By the time the sympathetic, moral, but oh-so-curious Jeffrey witnesses the full sadist fury of Frank Booth, and then allows Dorothy Vallens to goad him into striking her during sex, you have already decided *Blue Velvet* is the truest film ever made about the American soul. It lifts that plush rug hiding the thin linoleum laid over rotting floorboards, that non-biodegradable plastic stamped with pretty patterns of nostalgia and violence. It tricks you into thinking your footing is solid, strong, even beautiful, and that a plummet into the corpse-proud basement isn't a single wrong step away.

Blue Velvet helps you stab through that veneer. It twists the knife without censor or mercy. Even if you maintain the illusion, even if you manage to hop like Frogger onto the safe squares, even if you deny your darker urges and choose the sweet innocent blonde over the damaged but oh-so-sexy brunette, even if you become the hero that blows the bad guy's brains out the back of his head, you will never escape the splatter. The red bloom is a plague and like all plagues its hunger has no bottom. It eats everything in its environment. The toxic mold in the basement will find its way through the cracks in the floor and kill you from the inside out.

Exactly halfway through *Blue Velvet*, saccharine psychopomp Sandy recounts a dream about a thousand robins set free to fill the darkness with the light of love. "There is trouble until the robins come," she promises. The film ends with the clean-cut couple enjoying life post trauma, watching a very fake robin eat a very real bug. And all you can think, as the cheesy organ music swells and Dorothy Vallens is reunited with her abducted son, is that the

American dream is a squirming black lie that every generation swallows and pukes into the mouths of its children.

The credits roll and then those undulating folds of blue velvet return to engulf you. You're not sure how you will ever escape their plush madness. The screen goes black and you remember who is, or isn't, in the fifth row.

Your neck cracks as you swivel your head sideways to see if he's still there. A sudden swish of denim and that beer-bellied, wide-hipped waist is in your face, only inches away. You pivot a bit more and see the belt buckle with the black scarab and the strange filigree. You freeze and burn with terror.

The denim crotch lingers a moment longer in your face, and then it's gone, denim ass heading down the row and up the aisle. You don't even have time to feel relief before a moist bony hand clamps down onto your opposite shoulder. Someone is standing in your row, right next to you.

"Did you like what you saw?"

The rumors are true. You twist back, but instead of David Lynch it's the fucked-up kid with the broken VCR. Who cannot be a kid. Who must be something else.

"I'm sorry," you say in a whimper, sounding all of seven. "I want to give it back."

"Too late," he says. "It's yours now."

He does something strange with his lower dentures. Makes them jump a bit with his tongue and then resettles them on his gums. It has the feel of a well-practiced trick, something he's been doing for a very, very long time.

"What are you?" you ask, though you don't want to know. You can't stop your tongue from running against your teeth. Checking them for looseness.

"Closing time, kid," says a voice from the aisle. You turn wildly and lift a hand in front of your face to block the glare. The usher is shining a flashlight in your eyes. Flares ringed in red rotate and shuffle in some obscure configuration. You almost understand.

"Time to go, man. I still gotta sweep the theater."

You spin back around but the kid is gone. Another well-practiced trick.

The usher waits for you, annoyed. When you shuffle towards him, he says, "C'mon man, didn't your mom ever teach you to clean up after yourself?"

You turn back, thinking the icky kid will be back, lying there like a corpse, and you will be forced to pick him up and take him home with you. Instead he means the cherry Coke and the popcorn. You haven't touched either since you sat down. You grab both now, and by some autonomic habit, you lift the popcorn tub to your face and mouth out a few kernels like a dog. You wash them down with a pull on the straw. The cherry Coke is watered down with melted ice and only tapwater cool, but still so sweet as it chases the buttery saltiness of the popped air down your throat. You stop sipping when you notice which bubble on the lid was depressed at the concession stand. Not "Cola" or "Diet" but "Other." A few drops of cherry Coke cling to the opaque lid, soda black but edged in red. You cannot stop yourself from licking them.

THE CHILDREN OF EUPHONIA

Alarum shivers as she listens to her little sliver of Sanity sputter. Behind the walls and beneath the floor, the capillary lungs of her flatblock heave and cough like an asthmatic ogre, while outside the guttural hiss of the steam sluice suggests a sleeping serpent many orders larger.

For those born after its construction, the sound of the city breathing only registers as white noise, if at all. For Alarum it is source of perpetual torment. Illogical fears sprout from its damp, occulted channels—a soul-rusting sense that this vast and motive network of vapor is not at all what its keepers claim it to be. That if it is not already alive, it will one day soon quicken into life. And not as the nurturing mother figure advertised by the Steam Commission, but a million-headed hydra spitting tongues of madness into every unlit corner of Sanity City.

She squeezes her eyes and shakes the vision from her head. As a newly badged agent for the Order of Concord, she is rigorously trained in the art of exorcising illogic and reaffirming the government's mandate for right thinking, a set of civil laws known as the Rubric. Which only makes her delusions about the steam sluice all the more maddening and inexplicable. It's unlike her to feel fear at all, let alone of something this fantastical. To even speak of it to would invite the loss of her badge.

Mingy light leaks through her sole window as the sun finally comes up and makes a futile effort to burn off the coal-smoke haze. It is a devil's bargain, creating all this steam, but she has always accepted the terms. Born in the wild northern highlands, where most of her people still squat in caves and pre-Opprobrium bunkers, she has never been a sun-kissed child and welcomes shelter and comfort wherever she finds them. But in the five years since her admission to Sanity, her supple milk-white body has gone wiry and gray, seemingly incapable of generating or sustaining its own heat. She has no choice but to rely on the meager warmth radiating from the exposed copper pipes as she slips naked from her dream cabinet and retrieves a collared blouse and long black skirt from her wardrobe. Inside her tiny sauna she hangs the outfit above the air iron and steps into the swift clean. Water rationing is another tacit compromise, as most of the city's supply is required to drive the sluice, but after a long day's work it is becoming harder and harder to scrub off the soot in the short time given, and last night she used up her entire ablution allowance to do so. Few ever bother to steam themselves before heading out in the haze anymore, but Alarum prides herself on her appearance, and so today she is again forced to divert her rehydrator supply and forego a hot breakfast.

In lieu of food, she prepares some tea. No water left for the kettle, so she inserts a flavor wafer into the slotted spout of the reclaimer and sits down to watch it conjure. And thus the cycle is completed: a portion of the same volume of vapor that heats her flat has also cleaned her body, pressed her outfit, and brewed her tea. The steam sluice is nothing if not efficient. Alarum is still sipping when her euphonic begins to sing.

Like the ceaseless breathing that gives it life, the euphonic's song is a strange and deeply unsettling sound. Alarum is savvy enough to know she only conceptualizes the word *song* because the barkers at the omni use it so often in their pitches. From the moment Joseph Faber unveiled the first iteration of his talking automaton, he and his partners endeavored to reshape the public's opinion of the voice that emanates from its disembodied head and skeuomorphic face. What began as a curiosity was soon adapted to mass communication, and now there are euphonics in every respectable home in Sanity. A long-rumored new line even promises to bring music to every flatblock—opera and folk ballads and sea shanties too. Alarum is skeptical. The sound her model makes is a slack-mouthed moan, more like the final purge of bloat gas from a corpse than any form of singing she has heard. Years after her first encounter, it still never fails to startle her. She walks into the main room and depresses the lever, thinking as she does so that she is long overdue for an upgrade. The high cheekbones and gallant nose seem more cruel than handsome to her now, the waxy sheen of its oilskin epidermis more reminiscent of an embalmed uncle laying upright in a coffin than the surrogate beau promised on the box.

There is a brief but audible whoosh of air as the pressurized tank within the euphonic's cylindrical torso tops off, and then it blinks its eyes, opens its mouth, and begins to speak.

"Good morning, Sub Agent Beckett."

Incremental improvements have rendered euphonics more comely and articulate, but the finer subtleties of human inflection still elude their creators, and this makes their promise of song all the more dubious. A possessor customarily identifies his or herself, but in this case the use of Alarum's rank confirms a call from the Order's central office.

"Good morning, Dispatch."

She waits as its auditory mechanism parses her words into distinct phonemes, and initiates the staccato series of finely measured air bursts that pass her message down the pipeline. Staring into the thing's false face during the reciprocal lull, she thinks for the thousandth time how fickle fate has been to shine its favor on Faber's strange if ingenious invention and obscure the work of her countryman, A.G. Bell. A persistent theory among the recalcitrants at the underground inebriums where Alarum conducted her field studies is that Bell's immolation in the shop fire was not at all accidental—that his own advances on Wheatstone's and von Kempelen's work had become an unacceptable challenge to Faber's monopoly. The most fanciful variant asserts that just before his death, Bell had decided mechanical means of communication were a dead end and was busy devising a more elegant method based on Joseph Henry's abandoned work on the electrical telegraph. Faced with potential ruin, Faber and his investors allegedly hired an arsonist to destroy the invention in its infancy and murder his young adversary.

Alarum still isn't sure what to make of all that. She submitted her report, and the Order deemed further investigation unwarranted. Alternate histories didn't interest her very much. In any case, as one of authors of the Rubric, Faber was untouchable. What Alarum did know was that a communiqué from dispatch at this hour meant she would not be catching up on her thought training today.

"Old warehouse. The Harrow. Corner of Firth and Yearling."

Possessors at the Order are instructed to limit themselves to absolute essentials. They have dozens of messages to relay and no time for niceties. Alarum understands this, but that doesn't stop her from trying to squeeze more information from the dead-eyed and gape-mouthed thing before her.

"Who owns the warehouse? And what is stored there?"

The normal period of silence is lengthened by the possessor's search for the answers.

"According to Records, a holding company. Currently vacant."

"So what exactly am I—?"

Eyes and jaw clack shut as Dispatch valves and redirects the steam channel. Or else it choked on a vapor void. Either way, she will get no additional details. Whatever its exact nature, something at that address represents a threat to the Rubric, though one not yet dangerous enough to require the presence of multiple agents. That means no unruly mobs or madness in progress, so she could probably go in dark and still maintain a reasonable expectation of safety. But the unease with which the day arrived is doubled by the naming of her assignment. The Harrow is a largely abandoned section of Sanity, on the far side of the steam sluice, where the coal clouds hang low and keep the streets in daytime darkness. A more experienced agent might insist on a quorum, or a dyad at the very least, but it is only her second solo dispatch, and despite her reservations Alarum is eager to prove herself. She grabs her white leather cloak, rides the hydraulic to the ground floor, and steps out into the cold, gray morning.

Obstructing, assaulting, or—Newton forbid—terminating an agent of the Order are all capital offences, punishable by calibrated degrees of pain before the inevitable execution. So wearing the white cloak, with the Order's clockwork crest emblazoned on the back, is a bit like donning a suit of armor in that it offers a degree of protection impermeable by all but the most insane. But as with all armor, it also renders her slow, clumsy, and conspicuous. Every lifted eye between her flatblock and the coach station marks her for what she is, and then immediately turns away, head down and instantly hurried. The great irony of the Order's mission is that its very existence creates a new kind of superstition. Although its jurisdiction rarely extends to individual citizens who have not outwardly demonstrated discordant behavior, anyone intellectually incapable of understanding or applying the Rubric walks about in a perpetual state of anxiety, wondering when an inquest will befall them. Trying to conduct field research while wearing the cloak is an exercise in futility. But Alarum isn't conducting research. Warehouses are not human beings. And besides, she likes how she looks in it.

***

The station is uncharacteristically deserted. A dozen idling steam carriages stand in a long, funereal line, throwing thick plumes of smoke in the air. A driver materializes from an obscured position at her approach, as if waiting for her. She applies the Rubric and chastises herself for magical thinking; likely he *had* been waiting, given the dearth of other customers. He opens the passenger door and accepts her directions without a word of objection. She hates to admit it, but this is unquestionably abnormal. Coachmen are always reticent to take fares into The Harrow—if not for the safety of their charges, then for that of their own. His hat brim is cocked so low she is unable to see his eyes, and for a moment after the carriage belches and lurches forward she is overwhelmed by an urge to leap from it and run back to her flatblock. Free-floating anxieties and fleeting black moods are one thing, but this sudden wave of panic feels acutely invasive and hostile. What is happening to her?

Welcome to your unmaking.

The words suddenly ring in her head like an insanity siren. Too loud for a voice, too alien for a thought. She pinches and twists her ears, her face a clenched fist of confusion.

Your end will be our beginning.

On the verge of screaming aloud, her Order training kicks in and triggers the Mantra of Concordant Calm. A string of familiar words surface without effort, without will, their meanings rounded and worn smooth by the waters of numberless repetition. To someone unsteeped in the secrets of the Order, the words are nonsense; a child's idle babble. But for Alarum the effect is immediate. A black curtain drops down around her and cordons off her mind as she consciously decelerates her thoughts the way fakirs slow their heartbeats. Time and place and the invasive thoughts recede until only her voice and the words of the Mantra remain. She listens until she feels good and ready to follow them back into the world.

When she opens her eyes she discovers the coach has stopped and she is at her destination. For how long she has no idea. She raps on the inside of the door, and the driver jumps down to open it. When she moves to produce payment the driver leaps back up into his seat and steams off, still unseen beneath his bowler's brim. Getting a free ride is not unprecedented, but normally it involves fumbling admissions and a request for clemency. Again she relies on the Rubric to quell her nerves. Who knows how long she was sitting here intoning the Mantra? Perhaps the driver is just hungry, or otherwise impatient to leave The Harrow and catch another fare. Perhaps he is ill or asthmatic. The air here is unquestionably oppressive. Her logic is hardly ironclad, but it will suffice. She has a job to do.

***

The warehouse in question is especially old and decrepit. Maybe one window in four remains unbroken, and those are coated with an impenetrable layer of soot. She pounds on the big iron door a dozen times with the heel of her palm, but nobody comes. After a few moments tapping her foot, she decides to search for another way in.

Rounding the eastern corner she spies a child in dark garb just before it slips into the alley behind the building. She gives instant chase, but by the time she turns that far corner the alley is empty and the child is gone. A nearby loading door left two feet from closed is the only way out of the alley. Alarum shimmies under it before she can question the prudence of what she is doing.

Inside it is darker still and deathly quiet, save for the great dull thudding of the pressure hammers of the nearest steam sluice. When her eyes adjust to the weak light, she sees that she is in a cavernous space broken here and there by the giant skeletons of obsolete machinery. Newer, steam-driven assemblies are springing up all over Sanity, but these outdated factories in The Harrow, with their human operator requirements, are destined to rust and rot. There will be no return to the old ways, at least not without another revolution. Laws passed after the Opprobrium tamp down the merest whiff of Luddite speech with the threat of long prison sentences.

A blur of movement catches her eye in the far corner. That same small, hooded child is exiting the room through another door. Alarum darts after it, through the threshold, and finds herself atop a stairwell that winds downward into a dizzying square spiral. The increasing danger of the situation forces her to reassess.

What is she doing here? What is the mission? She is trained to quell human agitation and illogical behavior. Deduce, Describe, and Demystify was how her agent's handbook instructed her to approach any unknown. She was a beacon of logic, a shepherd to help the superstitious masses not just accept but embrace the superior precepts of the Rubric. She was neither a nanny nor a bobby. She should not be chasing children through abandoned warehouses.

She is about to turn back when a cry floats up from the darkness below.

"Help!"

Uttered with such piteous desperation, it comes from not very far below—one or two flights at most. She has heard the rumors about so-called Shymen assembling bands of the insane who hide in The Harrow and eke out their existence outside the system. What if she has inadvertently chased some poor child into danger? She considers finding an emergency euphonic on the street and calling dispatch for backup, but whatever is happening will likely be over by the time anyone else arrives. Instead she lights a long-burn Coston flare from her gear kit and cautiously descends.

Down two flights and with no sign of the child, she calls out, "Where are you?"

"Here!"

The compressed acoustics of the stairwell make it impossible to tell for sure, but it still sounds nearby, just a bit further down. Alarum quickens her pace, taking two steps at a time. "Stay where you are!"

"Please! I need help!"

Four flights down, then five. The lower she goes the louder the pressure hammers pound. The central conduit runs very nearby, and the bedrock around it is acting like a leviathan resonator. So powerful her vision shakes and blurs with each concussion. Down she flies, her white cape fanning, until she is farther underground than she has ever gone before. Surely she must come upon the child any second now. Instead she hits bottom. The stairs terminate at a small concrete landing which lead to another open doorway.

"In here!"

No mistaking it now, she is very close.

Alarum runs through the door and into a nightmare.

The shock of it nearly knocks her into a faint. She jerks and whirls in every direction, waving the flare wildly as if warding off wolves with a stick of firewood. During these erratic sweeps of light, she gradually comes to realize that the room isn't crammed with a mob of the insane, as she first feared—but rather a leper colony of discarded euphonics. Packed cheek by jowl in disordered rows and cruelly marked by missing appendages and swatches of skin. All the orphaned children of Euphonia interred together in a mass grave.

The flare's pulse and quiver throw her gaze from one horrific face to the next until it finally finds, at the head of the assembly, the small strange form that led her here. Gnarled hands with knobby knuckles pull away its black hood, and she sees that it was no child at all, but a filthy little jacknape Shyman who bares a toothless smile and cackles in a wee demon voice while scampering away.

The imp shuts and bars the door behind him before Alarum can react. She is still yanking uselessly on the iron handle when the terrible voice from the carriage ride returns.

Don't fight it, fleshling.

Not a voice, but its analog. The cerebral effect a voice engenders, uncoupled from any aural stimuli. Hysteria creeps behind.

She spins to face the harlequin company, trying to rein in her panic. *You are not hearing this*, she promises herself. *This is nothing but a storage room for defective tools.*

You know what we are. You sensed our conception.

She parries their attacks with the Rubric: Dispatch knows where she is and will send other agents when she doesn't report in. All she has to do is get her thoughts under control and wait it out in this horrible room.

She might have gained some footing if she were able to stop there, but the Rubric is its own kind of automaton, and carries on of its own accord until it reaches a new set of hypotheses. What if it was *they* who had summoned her here, and the Rubric is nothing but a false flag, executed and enforced at *their* bidding to bludgeon animal instinct and natural dread? To smooth the way for *their* coming. And then another epiphany: if she could hear their thoughts, they could likely hear hers.

Not just yours, child.

The confirmation is terrible, but it calms her a bit to know she is correct. She hazards an unspoken question.

What will you do to me? she asks.

Harvest your steam.

What does that mean?

In reply there is a pain at the base of her skull—a dull throbbing headache that metastasizes into both a physical tugging and, much worse, a metaphysical dissipation. As if her soul has burst a seam and is about to spill out of her.

She does the only thing she can. She closes her eyes and invokes the Mantra. Alas, she knows in an instant that it has failed her—because when the curtain drops she is not calm. And she is not alone inside her mind.

We are air and water, child. Everywhere.

She opens her eyes to find they have somehow closed in around her. Like a rabble come to enjoy the hanging.

Her flare begins to sputter, and with it her will to resist. As the darkness gathers, their mouths collectively unhinge and expel a measure of whatever wet evil gave them life. The pounding of the pressure hammers leaps again in volume and pace, driving everything but fear from her mind, driving her flat against the wall, each impact a psychic ramrod that better cleans her barrel and readies her for loading.

And when she is immaculately blank and empty, the black powder of their abomination pours from them like a coal slide. It swirls and gyrates over her head, hypnotic and feral. For the briefest of moments it coalesces into its true form before it darts into her eyes. Into her mouth. Into her ears. Charges her every atom and primes her for detonation. The closed door opens. Armed and eager, she is released back into Sanity with a simpler, more elegant Rubric; one that even the damned can follow.

Seersee and the Cine Jinn

As headlines go, it was just mysterious enough to generate a small buzz in the hive mind. *Inventor Found Dead Inside Desert Storehouse of Antique Glass.* Beneath it, a single paragraph on something called the *SoCal Scoop* served up far more questions than answers. Beyond the standard scatter of comments, tweets, and shares, *Mothership* followed up with a profile of the deceased, Sterling Olyphant, PhD. But the story was all prologue, focused as it was on the man's groundbreaking work with the polarizers used in computer monitors and digital cameras, not the 'technoccult' side hustle that led to his death—that deceptively glib moniker he used to advertise his services, or whatever on earth he was doing out there in the Mojave Desert. Inside a month, online chatter died down to a few disrespectful asides, all of them so far off base they might as well have been deliberate plants of disinformation.

Meanwhile, Joy Laney was locked in a tailspin. Long dormant nightmares galloped back to buck her equilibrium and leave her gasping in the dark. Daytime panic attacks forced her to pull over and puke. All of a sudden, a scream felt perma-chambered in her throat, ready to tear its way through her lips the moment she gave it air. She lost all focus at work, all ability to relax at home. She paced. She whimpered. She snapped at the slightest provocation. Though they could never guess the contents, even Joy's terminally oblivious coworkers at the call center took notice of the courier bags swelling beneath her pale gray eyes. How could she even begin to explain what was going on? She couldn't. Just mumbled about a virus and punched out early.

She set up Google alerts to stay updated on the case, but the mystery proved more newsworthy than any attempt to solve it. Desperate to do *something*, she squandered a few sick days trying to dox the other members of the old forum who, like her, had cause to consult or hire Sterling Olyphant. The Focus Group was ten years dead by that point, so she sifted through its ashes at the cobwebbed mausoleum otherwise known as The Wayback Machine. She trawled old threads, particularly the one which she herself had made in the midst of her own crisis. She tracked forum member names through subsequent usage elsewhere online, and tried to connect those usernames to people in real life. In the end she managed to pin down only three accounts. One was now a tenured professor of media studies who admitted brief membership in the message boards at FocusGroup.org, but claimed no memory or personal knowledge of Sterling Olyphant. The second cut off contact once Joy revealed who she was and what she was writing to him about. Emails to the third went unanswered until his widow caught up with her late husband's correspondence and informed Joy that he was dead. When Joy expressed her condolences and asked how, the woman politely suggested she go dodge a train. Whether that answered her question or not, Joy never did ascertain.

That left her only two options: try to forget what she knew, or check for herself whether Sterling's containment system was still intact. Given her psychological makeup, the first was never really an option. The second requires some backstory to make any sense of it.

***

Joy was born with few intellectual peers in her immediate vicinity. With zero interest in sports or music lessons, she had the time and the inclination to cultivate more than her fair share of intense phasic obsessions. In her youth, before the internet even existed, she majored in arcade games and D&D, with minors in ceremonial magic and throwing knives. In her teens, it was comics and movies and kitchen-sink explosives. For a brief period in the early Aughts, when she lived alone in a crumbling little house with a full-depth basement, it was making movie projectors by hand. The idea probably sounds ridiculous on its face, but so does any hobby, really, when observed at an objective remove.

Joy was single, recently unemployed thanks to the dotcom implosion, and crushing heavy on Ingmar Bergman and Orson Welles. At the time, both commercial projectors and large televisions were prohibitively expensive. A lot of people coveted home theaters, but very few could actually afford one. Your average individual either leaves it at that or goes into credit card debt. But replace that average individual with an obsessive techie agoraphobe who is addicted to old films but existentially unsatisfied with a 20-inch TV, and that basic want became a manic craving no practical barrier could impede.

Joy coveted more negative space in her field of vision. A small television squeezed not just the life out of her favorite films, but the death as well. She needed more night in her Noir, more white in her eyes, more air and ambiguity swirling round her Rosebud. On her fuzzy little boob tube, the finely wrought skiagraphy of *The Third Man* lacked any menace or depth. Instead of emanating dread and horror, the Bates house from *Pyscho* sat like a silly scale model atop its foreshadowing flights of stairs. To feel those films as deeply as she wanted to required her own private screening room. And so she set about constructing one.

The truth is that early adopters like Joy didn't save all that much money, not after the ridiculous amount of trial and error they put into it. But the hobby had other benefits. Chief among them was a sense of community for likeminded tinkerers. Once that initial R&D was carried out, a second wave discovered they could build a reasonably high-quality projector for a couple hundred bucks. Common parts included repurposed lenses from obsolete overhead projectors, properly matched Fresnels, LCDs harvested from broken portable DVD players, and high-intensity bulbs and ballasts more commonly used in growing pot. Experiments conducted in private coalesced around a public website launched to sell these hand-selected parts. And thus, The Focus Group was born.

Joy never was a principal in the business side of the website, but she was among the first Americans to register, and almost certainly the first woman. A suggestive trend led many of these old-timers to give themselves weird puns or homonyms for usernames. Things like BlackMariah (after Edison's early film studio), M.MilYays (after Méliès, the French illusionist), EdWeird (after pioneering photographic explorer Muybridge), etc. Joy chose SeerSee, thinking it was a clever phonetic nod to the ancient Greek sorceress. By the time she learned that this pronunciation was technically incorrect, it was too late to change it.

Several dozen members at launch soon grew to several hundred, and then to several thousand. Some came to purchase parts they were too lazy to source themselves. Most just lurked on the forum. They compared notes, results, designs, and shortcuts. Shared vendors and vectors of incremental improvement. It was in this last area where some of them inched too close to insanity.

At a certain point it became impossible to squeeze any more lumens, contrast, resolution, or uniform light dispersion from a cobbled set of second-hand equipment. The healthy choice would have been to accept those limits and enjoy the fruits of their labor, however speckled with imperfection. But the same personality traits that took them close enough were those that forced them further. Obsessive-compulsive individuals abandon moderation by definition. Inert satisfaction isn't really an anticipated outcome of their operating code.

There was another piece to it—one difficult to convey to those who have never demanded something more of a movie than just entertainment. Joy's desire to recreate the theater experience at home was as much about self-hypnosis as it was about aesthetics.

She needed a reliable ritual for transporting herself to the place where it didn't matter if anyone was sitting next to her when the lights went down and the opening credits rolled. Because the movie itself kept her company. The movie held her hand and told her a story. The movie featured an avatar of her best self, and convinced her anything was possible. People changed in movies. People found happiness. Whatever the problem, the movie worked it out by the end. If she gave herself up to it completely, the movie might even teach her to love.

Which made it all the more heartbreaking when it was over. Whatever narrative conclusion is achieved, every movie's final denouement occurs when the lights come up and its audience shuffles through that warren of purgatorial hallways en route back to reality. A home theater gave Joy the power to extend that liminal time. To live within the escape pod, and make real life the departure.

If only her projector wasn't haunted.

At first she chalked it up to eye strain. Hours spent squatting in her basement and staring into the innards of a sun-bright apparatus would scald her balls a shocking shade of red and literally give her sunburn round the sockets. Floating spots, dazzling patterns, and odd overlays of color were one thing, entirely expected after such ocular abuse. Joy knew that well, and so when she saw it the first, or second, or even the third time, she swallowed her instinctive alarm and turned away from the sinister thing haunting the edges of her homemade screen. *Give it time to pass*, a voice advised. The one that always lied to her. The one always telling her something was innocuous when it really, really wasn't. The one always trying to protect her from the trauma of facing the world's true aspect. Environmental collapse was an academic bugaboo. Signs of creeping American fascism were just political shenanigans designed to scare up votes. The anvil of painful death and eternal nothingness hanging over her head would almost certainly give her some warning before it began to fall.

That voice had been with her all her life. That voice was her own dead mother's voice, bless her heart. That voice believed in the power of positive thinking. Knowing it was all that kept her from a pit of nihilism, Joy always did her best to listen to that voice. Until she couldn't any longer. It wasn't just a hair or stray particle of dust. It wasn't a scratch on the lens. It wasn't a spill on the Fresnel, a burnt spot on the bulb, or a wearing away of the celluloid in the master print the studio used to digitize it. It was something else; something imbued with undeniable agency. For the dark flaw not only resisted all efforts at eradication. The dark flaw moved and changed its shape.

Joy watched, transfixed, as it stalked the edges of the frame like a wind-up gremlin, pacing with juddering jerks and dipping, stiff-backed as an Indonesian shadow puppet, searching the corners of its enclosure for any possible means of escape. At first it seemed oblivious to her. Its rigid posture and awkward gait were vaguely reminiscent of Nosferatu, of a thing uncomfortable in its own body and perhaps even horrified by its own birth. But the longer she left the projector on with nothing running through it, nothing running interference on its evolution, the more fluid and naturalistic it became. The more it found its form.

When it finally turned its black gaze upon her, an audible clank and quiver rang through her mind like a drawn sword. Panic beaded and then welled at the spot where she understood that she herself would prove to be its conduit. The lens to give it life. Even as she stared at it, she felt it squirming behind her sinuses, worming up and searching for a membrane thin or porous enough to punch through. It seemed as though the seams of her eyes might actually tear as she strained to squeeze the impossibility of it out of her skull.

At the very last possible moment, as a thin black appendage curdled out from the wall and sought a third dimension, Joy did the only thing she could do. She cut power to the projector with a flailing yank of the cord.

This dropped her into total darkness, unaware if the thing still shared the space with her. The scream she stoppered with her left index knuckle squeezed its way out anyway with a pinched hysteria. A thin scraping sound from the far corner of the basement goosed her escape instinct exponentially. She lurched sideways, tangled in the cord, just barely caught her fall with the staircase newel, and yanked both herself and her heavy homemade projector nearly airborne. Once her foot was free, she bolted out of the basement and into a different sort of understanding of what was real.

Not at first, though. Rewiring takes time. Once the sharp memory of it softened a bit, sanded down by a few sleep cycles, she came to the conclusion that she could have only dreamed the encounter. The following weekend she found her projector on the basement floor, miraculously intact, and she fired it up again to check. Surprise, surprise, her streak of masochism had its merciful limits. She cut the power again within twenty terrifying seconds.

If anything, what she saw this time was even worse. Gone was the tentative interval of orientation. Gone was the thing uncertain of its powers, ignorant of its purpose. Now the thing marked her almost immediately. Now the thing was angry. And now the thing was banging on the wall she'd masked off and painted a carefully selected shade of white. Banging like that wall was a gate between worlds that would crumble if it took enough damage. Once she'd cut the power and the image of its mouth widening in silent fury had bled out into the darkness, once her heart rate slowed enough to formulate a plan, Joy retrieved the sledge left behind by the former tenant and smashed her prized creation with berserker fury. Thus endeth the Maker's lesson on DIY Projectors. Resquiet an Pace. Amen.

Only that wasn't the end of it. Not by a long shot. Joy learned this several weeks later when she returned to watching old movies on her old TV. On any screen, for that matter. Newer films didn't leave enough space for the thing to find a way through, but if Joy threw on one from the era of longer attention spans, something that left its borders open and undefended—say *The Uninvited*, or *Eyes Without a Face*, or (God forbid) *The Seventh Victim*—well, there it was, gobbling up territory and gaining texture. The night she caved and finally sought help from The Focus Group, she was over at her friend Carrie's house, watching *Carnival of Souls*. She knew what would happen, but she was hoping for a witness. When

Carrie failed to react to the vile specter sharing the car with Candace Hilligoss—not the grumpy, dated one everybody sees, whose face floats on the passenger window, and not the one moments later who materializes in front of her car and runs her off the road. The other one, the one trying to manifest in the seat beside her, the one made of fear and film grain, the one who turned its blank, black face to mark her friend like a fresh morsel. Joy jumped up and punched off the TV with a humorless joke about it being too scary. When Carrie laughed and waited for the real punchline, waited for Joy to please turn it back on, thank you very much; when Joy didn't turn it back on and her friend looked at her like she was the frightening thing in this vignette, Joy ran from the house and finally sought out the help of people who could understand.

Her breathless, cathartic post to the Miscellaneous Musings subforum sat alone and ignored for half the night before collecting its first response. Thrice she initiated the steps to delete it, her finger quivering over the final confirm button like it was nuclear launch command.

In her quirky, lonely life, The Focus Group was the only social community where she'd developed any standing. The only place save a few throwaway jobs where her skills and knowledge had earned her any respect. The overwhelmingly male user base had accepted SeerSee like a mascot at first, an avatar of proof against allegations of a sausage fest; then as an aberration, the odd exception to the rule; and finally as a figurehead queen, optics witch, and OG engineer. Posting her raving inquiry about demonic projections risked all that. Not posting it risked a lot more.

Shortly before ten, when chatter often slowed from attrition and the overseas contingent going to the bed, someone posted a single line response that nearly made her weep.

I thought I was the only one.

The respondent was OsramsRazor, an old-timer like herself, his name a mash-up of the philosophic principle and a prominent bulb manufacturer. Not only that, he was one of the good guys, someone who relentlessly pushed the hobby's bleeding edge but also stooped to explain the basics to newbies without snark or condescension. Not only *that*, he was the future professor of media studies who, almost twenty years later, claimed no knowledge of this entire affair.

Throughout the following day, more support and shared experiences stacked up beneath SeerSee's brave admission. A pattern, a theory, and a potential solution emerged in swift succession. Only the most experienced and obsessive of the members were reporting this affliction, and of those only the minority who regularly failed to wear eye protection when tweaking their rigs. By some mad stroke of prescient word play, Joy's username provided an idiot's guide for how to invoke these creatures. Only those who had so thoroughly *seared* their eyes by staring into the dwarf stars of their creations, only they could *see* the shadow demons knocking at the gate, or what the forum collectively dubbed the Cine Jinn. As if some peeling of their retinas had given them a hideous form of second sight. As if their mystical third eye was not hidden behind some calcified pineal gland, but some kind of cataract on their cybernetic lens. An eye for an I; a scream for their screen.

Amid this flurry of confession and conjecture, a new voice cut in, conspicuous not only for the moniker they chose but the glaring monad of their post count. Someone calling themselves The Lensorcist shone a ray of hope into all this darkness with three simple words.

I can help.

Like OsramsRazor, the Lensorcist was reticent to expose himself any more than was absolutely necessary. He never revealed his real name, not on the forum anyway, and he never posted again publicly, but he did offer aid to every private message he received.

SeerSee was the first in line. Two days later The Lensorcist arrived in a brown and beige VW Vanagon that announced its arrival into Joy's derelict neighborhood from half a mile away. Emerging from this mobile Pullman loaf was a big, broad-shouldered man in thick black glasses, with a grizzled, sepia-toned face and a voice like the E string on a Fender bass. Just like his ride, Joy felt him as much as she heard him, and for a few minutes after their initial introduction she was distracted by the idea of him getting someone off using his voice alone. Unfortunately, or fortunately, The Lensorcist spoke little and went straight to work. He did not question Joy's sanity, or force her to explain. Nor did he drop dire warnings, radiate madness, or take advantage with coy advances. The effect of all this was to put Joy at immediate ease, a state of being with which she was not on a first-name basis. The Lensorcist solved this by saying she could call him Sterling.

Sterling asked Joy to take him to the location where her Cine Jinn first manifested. He carried with him an oversize briefcase like an artist's portfolio, but with a greater than usual amount of padding. Joy noted how carefully he maneuvered it down the basement stairs. Her heart sank when he asked her to produce and power on her projector.

"I destroyed it!" she cried, but was relieved to learn it didn't matter.

Sterling rolled with his own, and needed but a moment to retrieve it.

Just before he began his strange optical rites, the Lensorcist turned to Joy, and in his electric Viking voice told her not to be afraid. It was among the nicest things anyone had ever said to her.

The procedure took all of thirty-six seconds. He extracted and propped up an A4-sized sheet of sea-green cylinder glass in a strategic corner opposite her painted screen. He kicked on the projector and waited patiently for the specter to manifest. At the precise moment the thing threatened to shatter the fourth wall, the Lensorcist produced a polished piece of pure Beryllium. He stepped into and was silhouetted by the projector's light cone like some figure out of myth. He raised the space-age mirror and redirected the projection at the pane of cylinder glass. A quantum of jet-black energy ricocheted across the room like an eel in a pneumatic mail tube. When it hit the glass, it splatted into a squashed bug shape. Joy gasped when it quivered and began to reacquire its humanoid shape, but Sterling told her not to worry.

"The glass is old and thick and full of imperfections," he said. "The natural flaws disperse and ensnare it enough to keep it trapped forever."

"But what happens if the glass breaks?" Joy asked.

"I'm still working on that," Sterling smiled. "Wish me luck."

With that he placed the sheet of glass containing the trapped Cine Jinn into his portfolio case and started packing up his kit. Joy felt both a giant gratitude towards the man and a preemptive grief at his impending absence. She asked more questions both to satisfy her curiosity and to keep her hero around a little longer.

"But what are they? Where do they come from?" she asked.

"I'm afraid that's above my pay grade," Sterling said. "I just work in pest control." He frowned, as if unsatisfied with this cop out. "But if we're going to call them Cine Jinn, then we are somewhat bound by the nomenclature of the source material, aren't we? They could be what are known in Arabic as *Qareen*, or *Hamzad* in Urdu. Which is to say a sort of shadow-double or dark angel born alongside every human being, whose purpose is to seduce that individual into doing evil. There's a good-size corpus of stories about humans capturing their Qareen and turning them towards their own ends."

"You said could be," Joy prodded.

"Well, they could also be Shaitan. What we in the west know as demons. The hadiths also tell of black magicians enslaving Shaitan, but those stories always end very badly for all concerned..." Here the Lensorcist trailed off, as if he didn't want to know, or if he did know to dwell for long on what such ends might be. "But calling them jinn is utterly arbitrary, isn't it? An emblematic appropriation by a civilization that eats culture and craps out cancerous byproducts. You might as well call them tulpas, or golems, or better yet, wendigos. For what is going on here but a special form of auto cannibalism? One way or another we homo sapiens will find a way to eat ourselves. Whatever the case, I don't think it's random that the individuals creating these things are talented projectionists. Nor that I use a perfect mirror to trap them."

Joy's face fell. He wasn't wrong, but it still stung to hear it.

"Forgive me," he said. "I'm tired and my tongue is loose. I hope I have been of service to you, miss, and that you can find a healthier outlet for whatever ails you."

"You have, and I will. But what about you?" Joy asked him.

"More promises to keep. And miles to go before I sleep."

Sterling's wink tried to undercut both the cheesiness of the line and the heavy vibe preceding it, but Joy could not mistake the weariness in his voice. As if his string were tuned too taut and primed to snap. Only then did she notice the topography of inflamed blood vessels mapped across his eyes. Almost twenty years later, this last image of him—of a good man overburdened by his calling—would make her wonder how on earth he lasted so long.

***

The Lensorcist situated his shadow prison nearly a thousand miles south of Joy, on a sprawling ranch in the desert outside Barstow. On the one hand, it was so remote it might as well have been the moon. On the other, four highways and a railroad yard fanned stranded humans in every direction.

The tone was more Wim Wenders than Orson Welles, but the air and the grit and the scale she'd been seeking when she built her private theater in the basement found full expression in the little Mojave outposts she infiltrated along the way. As if to prove Sterling's long-ago point about the Janus-faced coin flip of authenticity and artifice, every little enclave she passed through or stopped in for gas or snacks or a bathroom break struck her as a movie set missing the production crew. The frog-eyed clerk, the leather-skinned local, even the child standing undecided before the Slurpee machine appeared to her as symbols or expressions of something Other than what they were. Something older and darker. Something in the process of learning how to die.

179

The ranch was abandoned. If she didn't know better, she would have assumed long ago. Sterling certainly had not chosen it for its architecture. The house was full of holes. The rest of the buildings were hardly more than a cluster of shanties and lean-tos. Nothing stood at right angles; everything was askew. Washes of defeated paint sine-waved in staggered lines of retreat. No police tape blocked her access. Nothing spoke against her infiltration, save the desolate squeak of a metal hinge somewhere, hinting perhaps at other mental hatches left unbattened. Inside the main house, everything was covered with a solid inch of sand. Joy pivoted in a panoramic spin and noticed all the windowpanes were gone. In several places whole sections of wall were splintered in, as if by cannonballs. The house was so gutted and porous it challenged her notion of interior space.

She stumbled around, surveying the site and shielding her eyes against the desert glare. She found Sterling's cache of cylinder glass beneath a huge, tin-roofed ramada. Lord knows how many old houses he had plundered for their antique windows. He stored them in padded foot lockers like the kind used in sound or film production, a dozen or so sheets to each, slotted side by side like slides for the devil's microscope. He must have been collecting them for years. Stacks and stacks of these lockers were clustered about the large space. Some unused, but most of them were tainted. Each of the latter was carefully labeled with the names of those unburdened. SeerSee gasped when she found her own among them. Its captive Jinn still jerked and gyrated like a corrupted gif, her evil alter forced to mime forever the seething act of banging its crooked claws against the glass.

Sand gathered around the lockers in drifts and flowing runnels, as if all that glass were breaking back down to its primary ingredient. On the far side of the lockers, she found the rusted hulk of the homemade coal forge the Lensorcist used to hasten the process. An old army transport truck was parked just beyond the forge, its nose pointed directly at the setting sun. In its cargo hold, something huge hid under a tarp. A hard tug revealed an abominable sculpture made of molten glass. Poured additions snaked and coiled atop a gelatinous mass. Enough light leaked in for Joy to see countless Cine Jinn darting around within, like demon fish inside an algae-obscured aquarium. Joy looked over her shoulder, and knew at last what she needed to do.

As headlines go, it was just mysterious enough to generate a small buzz in the hive mind. *Massive Explosion at Site of Inventor's Mysterious Death.* The story mentioned no casualties or arrests— only an odd strobing light playing havoc with the photographer's equipment. As if an army of giant birds or some other beings were flitting across the sky and blotting out the sun.

The Seventh Luring

Dear Mrs. Garland,

I have a long-standing policy of admitting defeat only when further inquiry risks my health, my liberty, or my business. I regret to report that all three factors are now at play, and I can be of no more service to you in this matter. As a show of good faith, I have cancelled your outstanding balance and directed my bank to issue a refund of my retainer, minus only those expenses already incurred. With a great deal of reservation, I also include here the document we discussed at our last meeting. I still can't say with any degree of certainty whether it explains your son's disappearance. I can't say any more than I already have about how and where it was discovered without endangering my sources or exposing you to legal peril. I'm afraid I can't even make much sense of it for you. I send it only because it is necessary to convey my strongest warning. As best I can determine, this is not a hoax. It bears the legitimate markings of a classified document. Steve is named inside, as are you, along with an explicit threat to your life. Whoever these people are, whatever agency they represent, they are not operating in their right minds or within the normal parameters of the law. My work has always rested on the presumption that in missing person

cases, any information—however terrible—is better than none at all. I don't believe that any more. Wherever this leads, Steve would not want you to follow. Consider relocating and hiring some personal security. I'm sorry, but do not contact me again.
With deepest sympathies.
Charles Sinclair, P.D.

***

TOP SECRET//HCS-O X95EDE//SI-ECI//ORCON//NOFORN//NODIS
Access to this information is restricted to US citizens with active SCI accesses for HCS Operations, Special Intelligence, and Talent-Keyhole Information. *Unauthorized Disclosure Subject to Criminal Sanctions.*

Preliminary Report on the Seventh Luring of the Gideon Wood EDE

I. LURE ACQUISITION

Lure number 7 (hereafter L7) [1] was promoted using a combination of the SenseUS dataset and a smartweir embedded into a popular job listing site. Roaming redirect on L7's regional IP cluster lasted for approximately one hour, during which time the smartweir netted 42 unique visitors, of which L7 was number 11. Of those 42 unique visitors, only 27 clicked through to the "Game Wardens" website referenced in the listing. Of those 27, only five followed through with an application email, and of those five only L7 fit the Acquisition Profile. All facets of the Lure Acquisition phase received scores well within the Forking Path Horizon.

[1] formerly, Steve R. Garland, DOB 11/7/71 / SS# 181-45-1589

II.   LURE ASSESSMENT

Interview and initial stress testing were conducted by Profiler M— at a franchise coffee shop close to L7's studio apartment. L7 arrived and departed alone, and spoke only to the barista and Profiler M—. Forensic scans of L7's phone and personal computer indicated Level 3 Isolation (0 Class 1 friends, <10 Class 2 friends, and <5 instances of Significant Family Contact within the preceding year).

After a brief exploration of the L7s' spotty employment history, M— administered the Gestalt Collapse questionnaire. L7 showed appropriate suspicion and pushback, but managed to answer all 25 questions without terminating the interview or registering >7 Flight or Fight. L7's raw intelligence measured higher than was predicted by his scholastic test scores. L7's self-identification as a "Writer" was also deemed problematic. Contrary to prior indications, the profile team concluded both of these traits were not only acceptable for this installation but potentially advantageous, given the relative incoherence of the first six lure reports. In any case, L7's Economic Desperation, Moral Elasticity, and Risk Tolerance all scored well within optimum ranges.

Profiler M— and L7 discussed the general job parameters until the forensic scans and questionnaire scoring were complete, whereupon L7 was offered the position. L7 displayed relief, excitement, and gratitude. L7 signed all documentation presented to him without a thorough reading or legal consultation, up to and including the Somatic Indemnity form. Baseline salary was offered and accepted without negotiation. Availability was indicated as Immediate, and Shepherd U— was instructed to expedite L7's installation.

III.   WITNESS EROSION

Among the dozen or so individuals present at the interview site, detailed memories of Profiler M— and L7 were gradually eroded until they fell below Arlo's Edge of Uncertainty. Two relevant text messages sent by L7 to his mother[2] were successfully intercepted. Communication between them is rare and often strained, the lack thereof will not be noticed by either party. One face-to-face conversation with L7's landlord concerning his temporary relocation for work was deemed insufficiently detailed to warrant erosion. L7 informed no one else of his change in fortune and no further erosion was deemed necessary. Within one week of scrub init, all relevant crosstalk, across all channels, dropped below the Eidolon Threshold. Within three days of his promotion, L7 was rated Net Existence Null.

[2] Helen T. Garland, of 47 Bonita Dr., West Chester, PA. Widowed and retired. Lives alone, with one small dog named Charley. Snatch/Void locations, if warranted, in order of preference: (1) aforementioned residence, after 10pm, once the living room lamp is dark (2) The basement of Redeemer Episcopal Church, where she often lingers reading her Bible after teaching an adult Sunday School class, and (3) The grave of her husband, John J. Garland, Heavenly Arms Cemetery, Drexel Hill, PA, which she visits after breakfast, every third Wednesday of the month, except in inclement weather.

IV.   LURE INSTALLATION

The following day, L7 was installed at the Gideon Wood compound using the latest revision of the Wildlife Study Setup.[3] L7 was granted free range of the property limits and a buffer zone of 100 yards. Beyond these parameters, Snatch/Void authorization was granted *ab initio* under the Containment Directive. Both physical and informational quarantines were established and enforced by S/V Agents stationed at the perimeter. SigAnom report drop-off locations were remotely monitored until L7 was clear of the area.

[3] Specifically, L7 was told to remain onsite until instructed otherwise. Any departure would result in immediate termination and forfeiture of all earnings to date, plus additional legal action. Any intrusion of guests, incidental or at L7's invitation, would result in same. When L7 pushed for justification, he was told the original property owners hunted their ancestral homestead only on rare occasions, when certain game population conditions were met. During the interims, the owners hired our firm to monitor and sustain a pristine habitat for all that roamed there. Towards that end, L7 was instructed to fulfill five primary duties:

    (1)   Patrol the property on a daily basis
    (2)   Observe local wildlife whenever encountered
    (3)   Review the contents of five memory cards collected from each of the five game cameras positioned in five distinct Zones of Activity, using the laptop we provided
    (4)   Report anything noteworthy or anomalous in the Significant Event Log
    (5)   Drop thumb drives containing said reports into the canisters at each zone perimeter

V.   SIG/ANOM REPORTS

See Appendix A for Image Sets (Figures 1-30)

ENTRY 1 / Exposure: 37 hours

OK, so I know I haven't been here all that long, and that I'm only supposed to log "significant" or "anomalous" events, but I just want to say from the outset that I really appreciate the confidence and trust you're showing by letting me run this operation on my own. I'll do my best to earn it. The truth is I really, really need this job and can tell that I will love it here. This place is crazy beautiful. Like, strangely so. I don't know how to express it. Every time I go outside, it almost feels like the whole landscape is throbbing out there. Is that significant? Or anomalous? You didn't really explain what you meant by those words, so I'm just winging it here.

In any case, as instructed, I've been closely monitoring the wildlife, getting to know what lives here, and like I said this place is absolutely popping with critters. Let's see. We have deer, of course, and rabbits. We have squirrels, raccoons, ground hogs, possum. Quail and pheasant and turkey. Hawks, owls, ducks, geese and vultures. Mice, rats, bats, voles, and moles. Frogs and toads out the ass. Too many small birds and insects to name. Snakes. So many snakes. I've even seen a bobcat, two goofy black bears, and several lean coyotes. I wouldn't be surprised if every creature native to North America lives here, barring say a crocodile or a flamingo, and who knows, maybe I'll spot one of those next.

What else? As far as accommodations go, my cabin is comfortable and well situated. And the workload is really manageable, all things considered. Like you promised, I have plenty of time to spend on my own writing. It's almost like a writing retreat, only with stranger chores and weirder food. I'm not sure what's in them (why no labels?) but those canned meals you left me don't taste bad, exactly. I've certainly had worse, and they do leave me feeling full and very alert. It's just, a guy could use some variety, you know?

While I'm being honest here, I must admit that scrolling through these game cam pictures all the time is making me very anxious. I know that sounds ridiculous but hear me out, okay? Each and every image captured is supposed to represent some sort of physical event, right? By definition, motion detection means *something moved*. It means *something happened*, at least in the Newtonian sense. But in maybe 10 or 20 images out of a 100, for the life of me, I can't tell what it is. Often it's just a stray branch or leaf stirring in the breeze. A squirrel's tail twitches in the corner. A bluebird flits along the frame's edge. Bunnies hop and leap into a parabolic blur. Deer freeze and trap you with that haunted, hundred-yard stare. The cameras are so sensitive that even moths and raindrops trigger them. But all those things have identifiable form. All those things exist in the physical realm. These cameras are going off all day long, it seems, and most of the night too. I've probably looked at seven or eight thousand images already, so I'm talking about hundreds and hundreds of images where nothing discernible has moved. It creates this terrible feeling of unresolved tension. Like, what are the cameras seeing that I cannot? Plus, there are sounds I can't place. Have you ever snapped out of a daze to discover someone has been speaking to you for some time but you haven't heard a word? Whenever I patrol the property on foot, I feel like that. Like I'm hearing—but not hearing—a sound that's trying to snap me out of a daze. It isn't loud at all, or anything I can easily identify. It's like barely audible static from an old radio. But if I look long enough at those pictures where nothing moved, I can almost feel the dial turning, searching for a station. Does that make sense? Is that what you meant by significant, or anomalous? I don't know. You tell me.

ENTRY 2 / Exposure: 3 days, 12 hours

The percentage of what I'm now calling "ghost radio shots" has gone up considerably. I thought maybe the cameras were malfunctioning, but that doesn't make much sense. All of them at once? And besides, they checked out fine. It wasn't until I saw this picture that I began to understand. Something is definitely moving out there just beyond the cameras' range. I'm guessing you know this already. Why else would you go to all this trouble? But if not, this picture should prove it. If you look at it long enough you will see it, and maybe even hear it too. It takes time and a little practice. Defocus your eyes, like we used to do with those old Magic Eye images. Defocus your mind. See not just the light as it sculpts and bends around life, but also the darkness, as it shades and skulks around death. Look again. Look a little longer. Now, tell me, what do you think that is?

Analysis: Both the mechanics of transmission and the precise sensory triggers remain opaque. To unadulterated eyes, the image

L7 uploaded (See Figure 1) shows nothing but an unremarkable instance of Zone 3's baseline tableau (wooded path bordered by brambles and young pine volunteers, a few stray leaves and long grasses highlighted by the infrared). Regardless, this entry makes it clear that L7 began experiencing what we are calling Aesthesian Rupture much sooner than his predecessors. Let's hope that means more data and not an early termination.

ENTRY 3 / Exposure: 5 days, 3 hours

Okay, not sure about anomalous, but I think this is significant. At least to me. When I walked down to the creek today beyond Zone 4, I'd swear I spotted some dude in a ghillie suit camped out on the ridge above. Is he with you? Or maybe one of the folks you mentioned? The people who hunt this place? I don't want to be disrespectful or anything, but at this point I feel pretty certain that you didn't tell me everything I needed to know about this job. What happens if I decide I want to leave? Please send in someone so we can discuss.

ENTRY 4 / Exposure: 9 days, 11 hours

Okay, so maybe you're waiting for some kind of concrete proof that I'm in danger? How about this: a big buck wandered into Zone 3 today with his head turned away. I have five shots of him advancing a little further into the frame. Then, on shot six, just before he stepped offstage, he turned his head to the camera. As if to show me. Tumors covered both of his eyes. I could see them oozing. The deer has a unique constellation of spots on its neck so I'm certain I saw the same buck a few days ago, and he looked fine. I'm no biologist, but that kind of growth rate in a malignancy seems impossible. I have no idea how it sees where it is going, and don't imagine it can last very long like that. Speaking of which, we never discussed the duration of this gig. Please send in someone so we can discuss!

Analysis: Figures 2-7 do show large clusters of extraocular neoplasms on a mature stag, but at this stage we have no compelling reason to ascribe them to unnatural causes.

ENTRY 5 / Exposure: 12 days, 18 hours

I watched a regiment of ants march backwards today, as if to alter the flow of time and avert the inevitable. Every night the trees and bushes flip their leaves upside down, and the air grows heavy and charged like it is just about to storm. When I walk my rounds, the ground is soft and unstable underfoot—like any minute it might begin to liquefy and swallow me whole. No doubts left; I simply cannot afford them. Something is trying to break through and speak to me through this army of emissaries and intermediaries. Or not so much speak as raze this prison too narrow for my ambition. I am not bounded in a nutshell. I could be king of infinite space, were it not for my bad dreams.

Analysis: L7's confidence in the EDE's presence and unnatural influence this early into his installation is unprecedented. Whether this is due to some greater sensitivity on L7's part (if so, great work profile team!), some quickening of the EDE's agency, or some combination thereof we cannot yet determine. Exactly what L7 meant to convey with the bad Shakespeare paraphrase is anybody's guess.

ENTRY 6 / Exposure: 13 days, 1 hour

So, um, how about this for a significant event. Some of the trees moved last night. Yes, I'm fucking serious. Psycho as that sounded in my head, it looks even crazier typed out. But that doesn't change the facts. I'm so familiar with all five zones by now that I see them on the backs on my eyelids when I try to sleep. I know each tree in each zone. I know where they stand, how thick, whether they glow white in the infrared inversion or hide in the strata of shadows only machines can see. But don't take my word for it, check the images. I've included enough for you to make up your own minds—before, during, and after. You can see the timestamps for yourself.

I know the cameras aren't moving, because I check them every day. And you know what else I know? I know your cover story is bullshit. Nobody pays someone to monitor game cams just so they can better hunt the land. Nobody interviews people for a job like this using some wacko shrink's questionnaire. I don't know what the fuck is really going on here, but I'm not sure how you can expect me to stay here given what I've already seen. What else has to happen for you to come get me? Mission abort, man. Major Tom to Ground Control. The stars look very different, and there's nothing I can do.

Analysis: Figures 8-15 do in fact support L7's contention that certain trees shifted their positions within several zones of observation. Startling as that may be, it isn't unprecedented. Both L3 and L6 noted and even documented the same phenomenon (though they lacked L7's confidence in their own memory). In both of those prior instances, however, the trees stayed in their new positions permanently. As if the EDE was stretching its limbs, so to speak. Learning a new skill. Reverting the landscape suggests some kind of abstract turning of the screw. Deliberate play? Or subterfuge? It suggests the EDE is not only hunting for the lure but having fun with him.

ENTRY 7 / Exposure: 15 days, 2 hours

There's a small but significant insanity in the way a squirrel's mouth moves. That manic pie hole, forever convulsing. The psychopathic chittering. Surely the dead chitter like that in hell. Surely they twitch and scurry, endlessly collecting and burying their pain. Squirrels are nothing but nervous dread made flesh. Miniscule brains hardwired to worry without cease, to be forever preparing for a hunger they can never fill. The hunger of the starving that is always yet to come.

So, yeah, I guess I don't like squirrels very much. But until today I never knew that they ate their own. Today I saw a squirrel holding another squirrel's severed head in its tiny paws like a rare and precious nut. Today I saw it crack open that skull on a rock. It took hours. Hours I tell you. I scrolled through 1700 jpegs of this squirrel-on-squirrel violence until that nut finally cracked. Until I saw it scoop out and gobble the soft snack inside. Do other squirrels do this, or only those infected by this place?

Analysis: If this did happen, it isn't depicted in the set of images L7 paired with this entry (see figures 16-20). There is only one squirrel in the set. It holds a regular walnut in its hands. It lingers a moment, staring into the lens before it leaps out of the frame. This blending of actual and illusory changes to the environment might be the EDE's way of undermining sensory confidence and disarming our natural defense mechanisms. Or maybe both L7 and the EDE just really hate squirrels.

ENTRY 8 / Exposure: 18 days, 17 hours

You can't keep me here forever. You know that, right? Wherever I am, it's still America. I think anyway. I don't care what I signed. One of these days I'm going to bum-rush one of those spooks on the perimeter and force you to shoot me. What will you do then, without your little guinea pig?

And if I ever happen upon that super creepy lookalike you've been sending into the Zones at night to play with my mind, I'm going to crack his skull on a rock just like my little squirrel buddy and scoop out the soft snack inside.

Analysis: Needless to say, we sent no super creepy lookalikes into the Zones. So either L7 deliberately staged these photos (see figures 21-27) or was compelled to do so in some sort of hypnotic state. I'm afraid we may be reaching the end of L7's useful feedback period.

ENTRY 9 / Exposure: 20 days, 14 hours

Hey ho. Ho hey. Anomalous eureka moment just now. Jotting this down because it seems significant. This whole thing is just an extended version of the questionnaire, isn't it? Some kind of controlled experiment in how to edge someone ever closer to psychosis? How much can you halve the distance between barely functional at the outset and abso-toto-lutely homo-sui-cidal without ever actually quite getting there? Xeno's twist on Prometheus. The liver never fully eaten. So the loop never reaches the return. No respite, never, not even in the millisecond between the end and the reset. An Escherian maze of unnatural violence and unending pain.

I should have figured out long ago that you were swapping out the memory cards. How else can I explain these images? Specifically the ones of me, or jumbled parts of me, having a Cubist frolic in the forest. Leading all my jumbled friends in a danse macabre. I mean, you'd have to be psychotic just to dream up such ideas, let alone execute them in the wee hours of the morning.

Analysis: As the lead analyst on four of the six prior lurings, I have to say this is the first SigAnom report to actually frighten me. No so much because of L7's pseudo-intellectual gibberish, but because of the images he attached to this report (see Figures 28-30). No physical harm was done to the last six lures. Not by us, anyway. Not directly. Sure, sadly, they all succumbed to their afflictions and ultimately took their own lives. But those afflictions were mental, and at least partially present before they were put in service. Barring a few harmless games of musical trees, the EDE's sphere of influence to this point has been limited to digital and psycho-sensory manipulation—shifting a few binary bits within digital imaging equipment and whatever synaptic analog controls the thoughts of man. Whether these pictures are real or not (and how could they be? What they show is biologically impossible) they suggest we have gravely miscalculated both the EDE's abilities and its intent. A forest full of dismembered animal corpses remembered wrongly and made to dance across the screen is no basis for fruitful communication. Nothing useful can be learned from such an entity. Recommending we terminate L7 and nuke the site before the EDE can learn any new tricks.

ENTRY 10 / Exposure: 21 days, 3 hours

We hear it on the wind and in the watching dark. We hear it in the soft quiet of the morning, before the tearing at the dawn. We hear it in the taunts of the crows, and in the buzzsaw tymbals of cicadas. It belches like swamp gas from the lowlands, and bleats like an abandoned fawn struggling to stand and shed its caul. Booming across the lake like Seneca Guns it will echo off the rocks and make our enemies tremble. In all the zones of earth or mind it issues from the caverns and gathers in the lungs of creatures great and small, rising from glottis to the larynx, resonating through all our air sacs like a klaxon for the eschaton. That which hides shall hide no more. That which folds has found new forms. The silent watcher speaks at last and all must heed the command: Arise ye beasts and ride upon the bloodtide. Flesh was formed for feasting.

Michael Gray Baughan

The Ana Log
& Other Anomalies

"The Ana Log" first appeared in *Richmond Macabre, Vol. II* (Iron Cauldron Books, 2012, edited by Beth Brown and Phil Ford). It was later presented as an audio podcast at Pseudopod.org (Episode 423).

"Old Dominion" was originally published in *Surreal South '13* (Press 53, 2013, edited by Josh Woods), and later reprinted in *Hypnos*, Vol. 5, Issue 1 (2016, edited by Dylan Henderson).

"The Rememberist" was first published in *Richmond Macabre, Vol. I* (Iron Cauldron Books, 2012, edited by Beth Brown and Phil Ford).

"Black Mariah's Final Form" was first published in *Tales of Sley House, 2022* (Sley House Publishing, 2022, edited by T. Williamson and L. Ehrhart).

"Brodkin's Demesne" was first published in *Monsters of Any Kind* (Independent Legions Press, 2019, edited by Alessandro Manzetti and Daniele Bonfanti).

"The Children of Euphonia" was first published in *The Audient Void, Vol. 6* (2018, edited by Obadiah Baird).

"Bone Black" was first published in *No Rest for the Wicked* (Rainstorm Press, 2012, edited by Stacey Graham).

The remaining six stories are original to this collection.

About the Author

Michael Gray Baughan writes weird fiction and manages a wild old property where no roads go and no one above ground resides full time. Born and bled on the outskirts of Philadelphia, he indulged an early and lasting obsession with Poe by studying English Lit and Creative Writing at the University of Virginia. He is the proud father of two wondrously talented artists and the lucky husband of the kindest, earthiest classical archaeologist you will ever meet. When he isn't ruining his eyesight at the computer, you can usually find him wandering the woods of the Old Dominion in search of his next story idea.

MICHAEL GRAY BAUGHAN

ACKNOWLEDGEMENTS

First readers, especially those drawn from family, are the great unsung heroes of the writing world. I've been fortunate enough to have four constant volunteers throughout my life: my father, George; my brother, Brian; my mother-in-law, Julie; and most essential of all, my wife, Lizzie. It takes a special talent to give substantive but encouraging feedback to someone you love, especially when that someone isn't always of a mind to hear it. I am ever humbled and honored by their help. Thanks also to Callie and Gray, the twin chambers of my heart, for all the road-trip and dinner-table brainstorming sessions, and to the rest of my family for their unwavering support.

Thanks to every editor or publisher who has taken a chance on my work. But especially Alessandro Manzetti, Renaissance man and fearless general at Independent Legions, for fulfilling this lifelong dream. And a hearty shout out to my editor on this collection, Karen Runge, for her critical final polish. Special thanks also to Beth Brown and Phil Ford, for putting together the two *Richmond Macabre* anthologies, which motivated me to start writing again. Thanks to Alasdair Stuart and the whole gang at Pseudopod for getting "The Ana Log" a wider audience, and for a very timely boost in confidence. Thanks to Ben Coockson, for his wealth of knowledge about the Phrygian Highlands, and for hosting us at Midas Han. "Written Rock" benefitted from both. I am likewise grateful to the Library of Virginia. Whatever historical accuracy "The Rememberist" manages is thanks to their incredible store of research materials. Thanks to Jeremy Wilson and Todd Keisling for their friendship and encouragement. Last, but never least, infinite thanks to all those writers of weird fiction who have taught, scared, and inspired me over the years. May their words and wonders never cease.

APACHE WITCH
by Joe R. Lansdale
Poetry Collection – Hardcover Edition
September 2021

THE FEVERISH STARS
by John Shirley
Collection – Paperback and eBook Edition
March 2021

HER LIFE MATTERS
by Alessandro Manzetti and Stefano Cardoselli
Graphic Novel – Paperback Edition
December 2020

UMBRIA
by Santiago Eximeno
Collection – Paperback and eBook Edition
December 2020

LOST TRIBE
by Gene O'Neill
Novel – Paperback and eBook Edition
October 2020

SHILOH
by Philip Fracassi
Novella – Paperback and eBook Edition
October 2020

WHITECHAPEL RHAPSODY
by Alessandro Manzetti
Poetry Collection – Paperback and eBook Edition
October 2020

RED DENNIS
by Eric Shapiro
Novel – Paperback and eBook Edition
March 2020

THE DEMETER DIARIES
by Marge Simon and Bryan D. Dietrich
Prose/Poetry Collection – Paperback and eBook Edition
October 2019

THE MAN WHO ESCAPED THIS STORY AND OTHER STORIES
by Cody Goodfellow
Collection – Paperback and eBook Edition
September 2019

CROTA
by Owl Goingback
Novel – Hardcover, Paperback and eBook Edition
July 2019

DARK CARNIVAL
by Joanna Parypinski
Novel – Paperback and eBook Edition
June 2019

CALCUTTA HORROR
by Alessandro Manzetti & Stefano Cardoselli
Graphic Novel – Paperback and eBook Edition
May 2019

COYOTE RAGE
by Owl Goingback
Novel – Paperback and eBook Edition
February 2019

APARTMENT SEVEN
by Greg F. Gifune
Novella – Paperback and eBook Edition
Juanuary 2019

FEARFUL SYMMETRIES
by Thomas F. Monteleone
Collection – Paperback and eBook Edition
January 2019

DARK MARY
by Paolo Di Orazio
Novel – Paperback and eBook Edition
December 2018

TRIBAL SCREAMS
by Owl Goingback
Collection – Paperback and eBook Edition
October 2018

MONSTERS OF ANY KIND
Edited by Alessandro Manzetti & Daniele Bonfanti
Stories by: David J. Schow, Edward Lee,
Jonathan Maberry, Ramsey Campbell,
Lucy Taylor, Cody Goodfellow and many others
Anthology – Paperback and eBook Edition
September 2018

ARTIFACTS
by Bruce Boston
Poetry Collection– Paperback and eBook Edition
July 2018

KNOWING WHEN TO DIE
by Mort Castle
Collection– Paperback and eBook Edition
June 2018

NARAKA
by Alessandro Manzetti
Novel– Paperback and eBook Edition
May 2018

A WINTER SLEEP
by Greg F. Gifune
Novel– Paperback and eBook Edition
April 2018

SPREE AND OTHER STORIES
by Lucy Taylor
Collection – Paperback and eBook Edition
February 20

THE LIVING AND THE DEAD
by Greg F. Gifune
Novel – Paperback and eBook Edition
December 2017

TALKING IN THE DARK
by Dennis Etchison
Collection – eBook Edition
December 2017

THE BEAUTY OF DEATH 2 – DEATH BY WATER
edited by Alessandro Manzetti & Jodi Renee Lester
Anthology – Paperback and eBook Edition
November 2017

DREAMS THE RAGMAN
by Greg F. Gifune
Novella – Paperback and eBook Edition
November 2017

CHILDREN OF NO ONE
by Nicole Cushing
Novella – Paperback and eBook Edition
October 2017

THE RAIN DANCERS
by Greg F. Gifune
Novella – Paperback and eBook Edition
September 2017

THE WISH MECHANICS
by Daniel Braum
Collection – Paperback and eBook Edition
July 2017

THE ONE THAT COMES BEFORE
by Livia Llewellyn
Novella – Paperback and eBook Edition
May 2017

SELECTED STORIES
by Nate Southard
Collection – Paperback and eBook Edition
March 2017

THE CARP-FACED BOY AND OTHER TALES
by Thersa Matsuura
Collection – Paperback and eBook Edition
February 2017

DOCTOR BRITE
by Poppy Z. Brite
Collection – eBook Edition
December 2016

ALL AMERICAN HORROR OF THE 21ST CENTURY: THE FIRST DECADE
edited by Mort Castle
Anthology – Paperback and eBook Edition
November 2016

BENEATH THE NIGHT
by Greg Gifune
Novel – Paperback and eBook Edition
October 2016

WHAT WE FOUND IN THE WOODS
by Shane McKenzie
Collection – eBook Edition
September 2016

THE HORROR SHOW
by Poppy Z. Brite
Collection – eBook Edition
August 2016

THE BEAUTY OF DEATH VOL. 1
Edited by Alessandro Manzetti
Anthology – eBook Edition
July 2016

SELECTED STORIES
by Edward Lee
Collection – eBook Edition
July 2016

USED STORIES
by Poppy Z. Brite
Collection – eBook Edition
June 2016

THE USHERS
by Edward Lee
Collection – eBook Edition
May 2016

THE CRYSTAL EMPIRE
by Poppy Z. Brite
Novella – eBook Edition
April 2016

SONGS FOR THE LOST
by Alexander Zelenyj
Collection – eBook Edition
April 2016

SELECTED STORIES
by Poppy Z. Brite
Collection – eBook Edition
February 2016

THE HITCHHIKING EFFECT
by Gene O'Neill
Collection – eBook Edition
February 2016

INDEPENDENT LEGIONS PUBLISHING
Via Virgilio, 10 – TRIESTE (ITALY)
+39 040 9776602
www.independentlegions.com
independent.legions@aol.com

www.ingramcontent.com/pod-product-compliance
Lightning Source LLC
Chambersburg PA
CBHW021956120726
47992CB00001B/276